BRAGAN UNIVERSITY SERIES
BOOK FIVE

# WAITING FOR YOU

## GIANNA GABRIELA

# COPYRIGHT

# DEDICATION

*Amanda, Chasidy, Ebonie, & Katie*

*Thank you for helping me make this story all that it is.*

*Tiffany Landers*

*Thank you for taking no time off to make this happen!*

*To My Readers*

*Thank you.*

# PROLOGUE

## AMELIA KING

### *February*

I sit at the couch with my pajamas on as I swipe left on most of the guys on this dating site. I downloaded this app because my sister told me to. Apparently, I need to put myself out there because otherwise, I'm going to die old and alone; those were her words. The thing is, I don't want a relationship right now. I told her that too but she said this app is the best way to meet non-dating guys.

I guess that's exactly what I'm looking for.

No dates. No dating. No strings.

"What are you doing?" my sister, Elia, asks as she walks out of her room with her cheerleading uniform on. She was so excited to finally make the team after trying out two years in a row and failing. She kept trying though because she had to be a cheerleader.

"Just swiping," I tell her, showing her my phone and the latest guy to pop up on the screen.

She comes closer to look at the picture then takes the phone from my hand. "Nope. No. No. Absolutely not. Uh, wait, this one. He's cute," she says, her fingers moving quickly on screen and then halting.

"Wait!" I yell, knowing what she's about to do next and not wanting her to do it. The last thing I want to do is match with a guy who my sister selects for me. It's not that she has the worst taste, it's just that her taste is totally different than mine. The opposite really. So yeah, not my taste. "Let me see!" I tell her.

"Too late, I've already swiped right!" she exclaims.

"You're the worst!" I reply, still lying down on the couch and looking up at her as she leans over me.

"Anndddd it's a match!" she announces dramatically.

I shake my head. "Pass it over!" I tell her, ready to see who I've matched with—who my devious little sister has chosen for me. Funny I call her my little sister, we're twins. I'm only a few minutes older, but I'll hold that against her forever.

She tosses the phone to me and I catch it before it hits me in the face. "I gotta go," she says, walking toward the door.

I point at her outfit. "First day of practice?" I ask. Do cheerleaders wear their uniforms to practice? Is that a thing?

"Yes!" she exclaims, eyes wide in excitement.

"It's February though, isn't that late to start?" I ask, wondering why they'd accept new cheerleaders into the team at the beginning of the spring semester.

My sister sighs loudly, tired of having to explain things to me, I assume. "This is how they always do it because they start training the cheerleaders who will join them in the fall now while the travel team is off competing," she explains.

I pretend it all makes sense. "Why do you have to wear your uniform?" I ask. Shouldn't she be wearing sweats or something? I mean, they're going to be practicing. Doesn't make sense to use their uniforms.

"We all have to wear them the first day of practice. They want to make sure they fit properly and comfortably." Another thing that doesn't make sense if they won't be using the uniforms until

September but maybe they use it earlier. Who knows? I don't really care enough to ask.

I take in her appearance from her ponytail down to her sneakers. "Seems like it fits tight."

"In all the right places," she says, smiling.

"Well, good luck with that!" I tell her.

"Thanks. I'm really excited." Of course she is. Cheerleading is the one thing she's passionate about. It's actually the reason she chose Bragan University. That, and the fact that I was already coming here and she hates being on her own. She's never had to be on her own. We literally shared a womb and just about everything since then, except tastes and hobbies, obviously.

"I'm happy for you," I tell her, sitting up and getting ready to turn on the TV. "So what do you guys do again?" I ask, trying to show some interest in the things that interest my sister yet finding it really hard.

She rubs her hands together before she starts. "Well, we have competitions, that's what the travel team is focusing on," she tells me. She rounds the couch so she's in front of me. "And we also cheer for the football and basketball teams," she pauses, "just to practice," she adds, making sure I understand that cheerleading is a sport independent of cheering for other sports.

I nod. "Well, remember what Mom said about athletes," I start, knowing my sister knows exactly where I'm going with this makes me smile.

She rolls her eyes. "It's not like I even know any of them. We haven't even started!" she says defensively. "They won't even be there until later in the semester," she adds.

"Still, what does she always say?" I press, enjoying this way too much.

"Gotta stay away from them," she repeats my mother's words begrudgingly.

I clap, knowing it'll annoy her even more. "Good job! Now don't forget that warning now that you'll be cheering for them," I tell her.

She shakes her head and walks right out the door without saying another word. The moment the door slams shut I burst out laughing.

I'm about to grab the remote when my phone buzzes with an incoming message. I unlock the phone and find that the guy my sister swiped on has already sent me a message. I open it before I even have a chance to look at his picture.

**Him:** So, what brings you here?

## NICK HUNTER

### *April*

I sit on the couch of this full ass house watching my brothers with pride. Watching the day their hard work pays off.

I can't help but feel jealous and a little sad, which is selfish, but it is what it is. I'm jealous that my dad made college graduation a requirement and so I couldn't apply and be drafted alongside them. Sad that I'll no longer be sharing a house with these guys, even though they were a pain most of the time. The truth is that college is really all we had; we may never live in the same state at the same time ever again. And that disappoints me, more than I thought it would.

I look around and see the way they sit nervously in the living room with their eyes fixed on the TV, waiting for the draft to begin, for their names to be called. My attention focuses on three guys specifically. My brother, Colton. His best friend, Chase. And my best friend, Zack. I can't believe they'll all be gone and I'll still be stuck here on my own. I turn my attention to where Jesse and Zoe are, oddly enough talking to my dad and the other parents. I can't believe Jesse is leaving the team. Though I guess his goal isn't the NFL, it's to be a doctor and he needs to focus on that now that he's getting ready to go into his final year of undergrad.

It'll be a team core rebuild, basically, and I'll be the glue keeping it all together. Coach informed me that I was Captain and that now that my brother is leaving, I'm responsible for the Football House too, replacing one Hunter with another.

"Are you guys ready?!" Zack shouts just as the Commissioner walks toward the podium to welcome everyone to the draft. No one answers his question and I bet it's because everyone is on the edge of their seats. Anticipation is killing them. I mean, all you've worked for as a football player comes down to this moment. Even the guys not getting drafted tonight, like me and Jesse, know the importance of this.

AFTER A FEW MINUTES, THE CINCINNATI BENGALS, WHO HAVE THE FIRST pick, are finally on the clock. I sit there with a beer in my hand and look around the room. I take it all in one last time before things change. Because they will change, it's inevitable.

I watch my brother, the guy I've looked up to my entire life, though I'd never tell him that. Even though he's first pick material, he's sitting here at the Football House with his family and friends, choosing us over a bunch of strangers, though that doesn't surprise me. The Colton graduating looks nothing like the Colton who started at Bragan. We used to be more alike back then but people grow up. I look at the way he holds Mia's hand. I can't believe those two are getting married soon. Even though I miss the old Colton, I'm happy for the new one. He's less miserable now and I have Mia to thank for that.

My eyes travel to Chase, who sits mere inches from Mia and Colton. He's sitting next to a random brunette. I've never seen her before, but I don't miss the way she tries to get his attention while he just focuses on the TV. I don't even know why girls try to be around him; he never gives them the time of day. The dude's an ass. Always has been, so at least that hasn't changed. I'm not sure it ever will.

Then there's Zack, who's sitting next to me. Zack, well, Zack has a grin on his face and his girl, Emma, is seated next to him. I can't believe he's dating Coach's daughter. I don't know how he's still alive. Shoot, if it had been me, Coach wouldn't have let me make it to this day. I'd be buried somewhere in the woods.

I see Colton and Mia get up from the couch and head to the kitchen, walking past the parents. I wonder if they're nervous about this next chapter. If they think about what that would mean for the two of them, I wonder if he's got a knot in his stomach. I know I do.

Commissioner Goodell comes back to the podium and once again any chatter that was in the room disappears. We have first-pick material in this room, so we have to pay attention. I'm really hoping none of the guys here end up in Cincinnati.

Goodell starts. "The Cincinnati Bengals have traded away their first pick to the New York Giants in exchange for the Giants fourth pick in the first and second round. With the first pick in the 2020 NFL Draft, the New York Giants select Colton Hunter, quarterback, Bragan."

Colton walks back into the room with his phone to his ear and a smile on his face. "Let's go!" I get up from my seat on the couch and scream as I run over to my brother and embrace him. New York is only a couple hours away. "You didn't have to keep us in suspense, you know!" I tell him, knowing the phone call he just finished had to have been the reason they went to the kitchen earlier.

"I wanted to make sure it was actually happening," he says, shrugging.

Everyone claps and shouts and the cameras I've been ignoring since I walked into this draft party are instantly on him. Jokes on them though, this is about to be the most boring interview they've ever held.

So, I was right. The interview Colton had lasted less than two minutes and every word out of his mouth sounded as if he had been coached by Bill Belichick himself. That would've been a better landing place for him, especially now that they need a quarterback, but there's no way they would've had him at twenty-three and no way they could've or would've traded to get him at one. The draft continues with players from other schools being drafted. I start to feel the energy change in the room and I know it's because the guys who haven't been drafted are wondering how far they'll fall now that we're getting toward the end of the first round.

The Patriots are finally on the clock and I can't wait to see who they draft. They're clearly in desperate need of a quarterback, but somehow, I doubt that they'll draft one right now, that's too obvious. I look around the room to see who's still here. This wasn't an open party where everyone was invited. It was mostly the team and the parents of the players being drafted.

Everyone shuffles around, grabbing beers, water, and just distracting themselves as they wait. I just stay seated on the couch and take it all in. This will be me next year.

Emma and Zack walk back into the living room, both with beers and huge smiles on their face. "Let's go!" Zack shouts.

"What happened?!" I ask while jumping up from the couch.

He walks over to where I'm standing and throws his arm over my shoulder. "You're not going to believe me if I tell you, so you may as well wait and see."

I turn to the TV and then back to Zack's goofy smile. He can't be saying what I think he's saying. "You're not serious."

"Just watch," Emma says with pride in her eyes and the whole room is silent. Shocked. Surprised. Waiting.

The Commissioner steps back onto the podium and Zack's smile gets even wider. "With the 23$^{rd}$ overall pick in the 2020 NFL Draft, the New England Patriots select Zack Hayes, Left Tackle, Bragan!" The moment the words leave Goodell's mouth, I run around the room screaming like a crazy person.

I wait for Zack to hug his parents and I don't miss the tears in their eyes. "You're a Patriot!?!" I shout when he comes over to where the guys are standing.

Zack nods.

"Holy crap!" I scream.

"You deserve it," Colton says.

"Guess you're staying in New England," Chase adds.

"I'm definitely going to be your plus one for all the home games," I tell him.

Emma clears her throat and glares at me. I deserve that. She is his girlfriend, so I understand why she'd want priority. "Ah, I'm still here!"

"Eh. You can just read it in a book. I'll even write you a report if you want," I say half-jokingly.

"The Patriots, my guy, how do we feel about being drafted by the New England Patriots?" Jesse asks, doing his best impression of Matthew Slater.

"Like it's all been worth it," Zack says with relief visible on his face. He deserves this more than anyone I know.

"Hey buddy, was that Belichick who called?" I ask curiously.

"Yeah," he responds, rubbing the back of his neck.

"And?" I ask, grinning.

"Scariest phone call of my life," he chuckles and I laugh alongside him.

"Get ready for the Patriot's Way," I tell him.


THE COMMISSIONER CONTINUES AND WE SIT DOWN AND CELEBRATE while also wondering who'll get picked next. Colton is going to the New York Giants and Zack is going to the New England Patriots. Man, I wish I were joining them or competing against them at the next level. I guess I will soon enough.

I turn to Chase and see the worried look on his face. A look he's trying to hide but is failing. It's the look that comes from the fact that it's the second round and his name has yet to be called. He shouldn't worry though; he's definitely getting picked today. He's one of the best in the draft class.

As the second round progresses, the air feels a little more tense.

We all sit there with excitement buzzing at what we already know but worry creeping in for what we don't. The tension in the air is sharp. The silence doesn't help.

Then, a phone ringing echoes in the room. Everyone looks around to figure out where it's coming from. But my eyes dart to Chase.

He looks at the phone on the coffee table in front of him and picks it up. "Hello," he says and we all watch his every move and listen to his every word.

"That's great. Thank you," he replies. I really wish we could hear the other side of this conversation. I look at the TV and see that the Jets are on the clock.

I turn back to Chase and wait for him to finally say something else to the other person on the line. "I'm looking forward to it, Coach."

Goodell steps onto the stage just as Boulder hangs up. I look from him to the TV and back. Goodell starts to speak, "With the 48th pick of the 2020 NFL Draft, the New York Jets select Chase Boulder, Defensive Lineman, Bragan."

Same as with the others, the announcement is followed by shouting and hugs. "New York, baby!" Colton says, walking over toward his best friend and hugging him. It's a weird sight for most people, considering those two aren't really known for being huggers. Special occasions make people do special things.

"Guess we'll be seeing a lot of each other," Chase replies.

"We share a stadium after all," Colton says.

I get up and congratulate him. "Easy enough. I'll visit both of you. It's going to be fun watching you go against each other. Then all the Pats' games. Man, this is going to be great!" I say, my anxiousness being replaced with pure excitement. So many tickets to so many NFL games to hold me over until I get to be there myself.

"Damn, I didn't think of that," Colton says, grimacing.

"Please don't hurt him," Mia tells Chase jokingly.

"I'm not there to defend him, so you can't damage him," Zack adds.

Chase smiles, which I bet shocks everyone because he never does that. Again, I guess being drafted is the exception. "I can't make any promises."

"Football just got a whole lot more fun," I joke, then we party the rest of the night and draft away.

# 1

NICK HUNTER

*August*

"Get your asses on the field," Coach Wilson screams and I instantly put my phone away and get to it. It's August and with most of the top players, Jesse, Zack, Colton, and Chase gone, the rest of us are suffering. Coach isn't even letting us have more than the occasional water break.

I run over to where the tight ends and receivers are. "Hunter!" Coach shouts. "Hunter," he shouts again and I turn around, remembering that I'm the only Hunter on the team now. So, he's clearly talking to me.

"Yes, Coach?" I respond.

"Go work with the new quarterback," he replies, pointing at the new guy.

I nod and switch directions, walking over to where the quarterbacks are practicing with Coach Stevens. "Coach sent me here," I tell Stevens the moment I arrive.

Coach Stevens looks at me for a second too long; he's never really liked me. Then again, most people don't. "I need you to do some drills with Lincoln," he replies.

"Who's Lincoln?" I ask, just to be petty.

The new QB1 clears his throat. "Me," he responds.

"Oh, yeah, I can. What do you want me to do?" I ask Stevens.

"Just run different routes and catch the ball," he instructs.

I smile. "You know I've never had any issues catching the ball, just make sure the new rookie doesn't screw up the pass," I reply cockily.

"Shut up, Hunter," Coach Stevens admonishes. "Ignore him. His mouth doesn't do him any favors," he adds.

"Alright, let's do this," I tell them, ready to end this interaction.

We walk away from where Coach Stevens is going over the playbook with the backup quarterback, Mersier. He's been the backup for two years now and has never needed to play because my brother never needed him. He may have to with this new quarterback though, so he may as well be ready.

We practice a few drills and I've gotta say he's not half bad. Granted, we can't judge that on throwing some perfect spirals on an empty field. It's how he acts on game day that'll make all the difference.

Some may say I hate the new guy and they wouldn't be entirely wrong. I don't trust him. I don't trust this team to be good enough without the guys we lost. I trust me to kick ass but I can't catch if the passes aren't being sent my way. This freshman has never played a game outside of high school and he's somehow expected to take over for my brother. Mersier would be a better choice at this point.

This guy just came out of nowhere, surpassing our backup for the starting role.

I hate that.

Hate when guys skip the whole red shirt year and get right on the team. I mean, I did that. Still, it usually comes with a cocky attitude, I should know.

I can't even read him.

Did I mention he's already being extra weird? When we all arrived at Bragan for practice, he said he wouldn't be joining us by living at the Football House.

Even when we told him that it was kind of a requirement, he just shrugged it off. He didn't bother offering an explanation, just plainly refused to follow tradition. To do things the way they've always been done. So yeah, I kind of hate the guy. There's a room in the house for him anyway but it's just a waste of space. I'm about to start using it to store my practice clothes. That way, if he ever comes, he'll get a nice welcoming smell.

"Ten and out!" he yells and I do as I'm told. The football spirals right into my hands for a perfectly-timed catch.

"Good job! Let's call it for today," Coach Stevens shouts then turns around and walks away.

Lincoln heads over to where I am and extends his hand. "Good catch," he says.

I shake his mostly because the future of my NFL career sort of depends on him. "Good throw. Hopefully, you can do that in an actual game," I can't help but quip.

"I guess we'll see," he says knowingly, and then we're all walking toward the locker room.

The moment I reach my locker I pull out my phone. I go look through my messages and instantly find the one I'm looking for. The one that tells me she'll be back on campus in a couple of weeks. Good.

## AMELIA KING

"So, when do you think you'll be free again?" he asks as he finishes putting his shirt on. I stop myself from frowning at the fact that I can't see the muscles on his back anymore.

"I'll let you know," I tell him, half distracted by the mere presence of him in my room.

He turns toward me and gives me the childish smirk I've come to know. "Soon?"

I shrug. "Maybe."

"Alright, well…" he looks around the room, then his eyes find mine. "I'm out." He watches me for a few seconds then his mouth opens to say something. Thinking better of it, he shakes his head and walks out of the room.

It's 2 am.

He's probably going to a party or something. Somewhere else. With someone else. I'm not supposed to care though. I don't care.

That's the arrangement we have.

My door flies open, taking all my attention. Then, my sister saunters in with her mouth and eyes opened wide. "Was that Nick Hunter?" Elia asks.

I don't respond. I just look at the person I was forced to share my space with for the better part of my life. The deal was we stick together. We always have. Literally, since the womb.

We're twins.

Not identical. Not by far. She's all air and lightness. She looks at life through rose colored glasses. I'm the opposite of that. Mom never understood how two completely opposite people could have been made at the same time.

We can't even share clothes. She's all preppy. I'm … well, not.

She rocks skirts, dresses, and heels. I wear ripped jeans, hoodies, and whatever shoes won't make my feet hurt.

"This is the fourth night I run into him," she says. She walks toward my bed and is about to take a seat on it but then looks down and stops herself midway. Instead, she pulls one of the bean bags from the corner of the room and drags it closer to the bed before plopping onto it. "Are you going to say anything?" she asks expectantly.

"What do you want me to say?" I reply, leaning back on the headboard.

"That was Nick Hunter who just left our apartment. Again. Nick Hunter, the football player." I'm not sure why my sister is still shocked at seeing him here. I figured by now it would wear off. We started talking back in February. Met up in March and have been seeing each other randomly since then.

"Sounds like you have all the information you need," I tell her, not in a particularly sharing mood. Though I guess I never am.

"Are you two dating?" she asks, again.

"No," I repeat the same answer I've given her since the first time she ran into him here.

"Why not?" she asks, confused as to how I'd let him into my bed often but keep him locked out of my heart.

I stretch my arms. "I don't want to."

"YOU don't want to?" she squeals. I guess, in her defense, she likely expected him to be the one who wouldn't want to be tied down. I don't think she's wrong about that. But it doesn't matter what he wants or doesn't want because I know where I stand. As long as I'm sure, that's all that matters.

"No. I don't," I reply, my words sounding harsher than I intended.

"Why not?" my sister, ever the detective, questions. She chose a perfect career path in journalism seeing as she's always fishing for news.

Nothing to see here though.

"I've gotta focus on my studies. I don't have time for relationships," I remind her. That's another difference between my sister and me. I care about grades and classes. She cares about having life experiences.

Like I said... polar opposites.

"So, what? You just use him on the side?" she asks, getting up from the bean bag.

I nod. "It works."

"How?" she questions, her arms crossed in front of her, reminding me of our mother.

"We each get what we want without worrying about commitments," I try and explain, though I know it's futile. My sister doesn't do random hookups.

"So he sleeps with other girls?" She asks, disgust visible on her face.

I don't think he does. "He does not," I tell her, though I'm not certain. I hate that I'm not sure. Not because I care about him but because I care about me.

We always use protection but I don't like the thought of other girls... not one bit.

"Are you sure?" she asks, and I get up from my bed, tired of the direction this conversation has taken.

"Yup. I want some water," I say, walking out of my own room hoping to get a break from the interrogation that's taking place. I walk over to the kitchen as slowly as possible, hoping that by the time I return to my room, my sister has either forgotten about the conversation or just went to her room altogether.

# 2

## NICK

I run into Elia the moment I step outside of Amelia's bedroom. I take her in and smile at the striking differences between them. I think it's funny that I'm a twin hooking up with a twin.

"Again?" she asks. I can't blame her though; I've been hanging at her apartment more often than usual. In my defense, I hadn't really seen Amelia for a few weeks during the summer, so I had to make up for it.

"What can I say?" I tell her, smiling smugly.

She shakes her head. "I don't get it," she says, seemingly confused by the arrangement her sister and I have.

"That's okay..." I say, walking past her and toward the elevator. "It's really your fault for swiping," I say teasingly. She says something else but it isn't loud enough for me to hear.

I get why she doesn't understand the arrangement between her sister and me, sometimes I don't understand it either. All I know is

I'm basically sworn to secrecy. The only people who know are obviously Amelia and her sister.

I don't mind keeping it to myself though. The guys would never let me hear the end of it if they knew I was finding myself with the same girl, multiple times a week, for months now.

Also, Amelia would kill me if she found out I had said something to anyone about what we're doing. Total silence is the rule.

That was the plan.

It's not like we thought this would happen, the two of us seeing each other. I was just bored on a dating site. We had just won the championship and I had nothing better to do. I saw her picture, swiped right on it and it was a match. I was intrigued and sent a message, which she ignored for a couple weeks. I could tell she read it but chose to not respond. It bugged the hell out of me. But one night, I saw her at a party I had crashed and approached her. Funny enough, she later told me that was the first Bragan party she had gone to and only went because her sister convinced her to. The moment I saw her, I knew it was the same girl from the chat and I wanted to figure out why she was ignoring me; like I said, I didn't like it.

That night started everything.

We were both physically attracted to each other.

She knew what she wanted. I knew what I wanted. So, we left the party together and that was that.

I thought it was only going to happen once, like most of my hookups, but then I couldn't help messaging her again on the dating site and she finally responded. It's been a few months since that night and for the life of me I can't figure out how it ended up this way.

Well, I sort of can.

There's no drama with her. No hidden agenda. She doesn't want a relationship with me. Doesn't want me to linger or have feelings for her. It's like I'm dating a female version of me. I kinda love it.

We both wanted it to be a one-time thing. Mostly because I never see the same girl more than once and because she found out I was a football player and wanted nothing to do with that, though I can't imagine why anyone would feel that way.

Then again, she's prelaw and a genius. I'm pre-NFL and not the brightest crayon in the box if I'm being honest.

So a cone of silence it was. Except her sister saw me leaving her house one time with my shirt barely on and could immediately tell what was going on. Neither one of us cared enough to stop after she found out.

I reach the lobby and walk out with a smile on my face. The moment I step out of the apartment building that's conveniently a few blocks from campus, my phone buzzes with a text.

**New Guy:** What are you doing?

**Me:** It's 2 am. What do you think I'm doing?

**New Guy:** Partying? Drunk somewhere?

**Me:** You barely know me. I'm not doing any of those things. What do you need?

Lincoln doesn't just text me at 2 am for no reason.

**New Guy:** The party at the House is getting out of hand.

I thought filling in for my brother would be easy but people actually listened when he spoke. The same doesn't apply for me, mostly because I'm not as serious as he is. I don't like having to keep others in check.

**Me:** What do you mean out of hand?

I start walking toward my car and wonder how bad a party can get that I'm being messaged at 2 am to do something about it. ME, out of all people, and by Lincoln.

**New Guy:** One of the guys texted me and said the hockey team is there and being rowdy.

**Me:** Why not just text me directly?

I ask him, wondering why the guys would send Lincoln a message when he doesn't live at the House and doesn't show up to the parties.

**New Guy:** They did.

He replies and when I scroll down I see all the messages I've missed. All about the hockey team. The bane of our existence. These guys have decided that now's the time to mingle with the football team. They're a bunch of savages and usually, when they show up, all the furniture that isn't moved to the basement ends up broken.

Turning on the car, I drive the short distance to the Football House ready to kick people out.

## AMELIA

I TWIST AND TURN IN BED ALL NIGHT UNTIL I FINALLY GIVE UP. SLEEP IS not happening today and it's all thanks to my sister. Whenever I close my eyes, I can't help but think about her words.

*Are you sure?*

Am I sure that I'm the only one he's currently seeing? That's what she was asking. I said yes to her but the reality is that I don't know. Every second I spend lying on this bed is more time I spend thinking about him.

About other girls.

About him and other girls.

I'm not jealous. Not one bit. I don't care.

The reason I talked to him at that party isn't that I was looking for someone to fall in love with. Actually, it was the complete opposite.

I was looking for someone I could get what I wanted from and nothing more.

He isn't the relationship type. He's not my type.

He's a temporary person in my life who I won't miss when I move on to the next chapter.

But still, the thought of other girls bothers me.

I sit up in my bed and look at the clock. 5 am. He left my house at 2 am and it was almost 3 am by the time I actually settled into bed.

Luckily, by the time I came back from getting water, my sister was out of my room and left me alone with the questions she had put in my head.

I turn to the side and grab my phone from under my pillow. Unlocking the phone, I do something I've never done before. I prepare myself to send a text that may give him the wrong impression.

**Me:** Are you sleeping with other girls?

I send it and hate that it sounds like I'm jealous.

**Me:** If you are, it's fine. I'm not jealous or anything. I just would like to know.

I send a follow-up text and cringe the moment I press send. I don't know if I'm making it better or worse. Still, if he's sleeping with other girls, then our arrangement is done.

Surprisingly, I see the three dots indicating he's typing. I guess he didn't get much sleep after he left either.

**Football Player:** Are you sure you're not jealous? ;)

His answer doesn't surprise me. I have to admit I sound like a jealous girlfriend.

**Me:** Not jealous. I just want to know I'm not at risk of being given something I don't want.

**Football Player:** Like what?

**Me:** Have you ever taken a health class?

**Football Player:** I think so... just never paid any attention really.

I roll my eyes then type up the next reply.

**Me:** So, is that a yes on sleeping with other girls?

**Football Player:** Are you sleeping with other guys?

**Me:** Why does that matter?

The answer is no. Plain and simple. I don't want to be in a relationship with other guys. I don't need other guys. I get what I want from Nick and that's that.

**Football Player:** You're asking me... you should answer the same question.

**Me:** I asked you first.

**Football Player:** I want to know before I answer.

**Me:** Would you even care if I were?

**Football Player:** ...

**Me:** What does that mean?

**Football Player:** I'm trying to think about whether I care...

I cannot stand him. Still though, I keep him around. It could've been and should've been a one and done type of thing. I don't know how I've convinced myself to keep it going. I guess Nick deserves a little credit for that.

**Me:** You shouldn't.

**Football Player:** Do you?

**Me:** I care for specific reasons...

**Football Player:** We've been sleeping together for a few months now and this question has never come up. Why now?

**Me:** I hadn't thought about it until today.

I reply to him honestly. If it weren't for my sister, I would've gotten a great night of sleep and wouldn't be talking to Nick at the crack of dawn.

**Football Player:** You falling for me?

**Me:** Keep dreaming.

**Football Player:** I'll just keep waiting for you to.

**Me:** So, are you just not going to answer the question?

**Football Player:** You first.

**Me:** You're being childish.

**Football Player:** So are you.

**Me:** Why are you this difficult?

**Football Player:** I can be easy if you want. ;)

# 3

## NICK

I'm lying in bed tired as hell. The party ended 45 minutes ago and for the life of me I can't remember why I once wanted to throw a party every weekend. Party every time we win a game... that's what I said. Somehow, the guys thought it would be smart to start partying before we even have our first game. I don't think I can handle another party next weekend. The moment the thought enters my brain I realize I'm starting to sound just like my brother.

He'd be pissed at the mess from tonight. The hockey team is a mess when they party. Tonight, they broke the only table the guys were too lazy to move into the basement. It's still crazy to me that I had to come to the party and lay down the law. I had to come in and pretend to be a strict guy, though we all know that's not really me. I kicked their asses out of our House. Eventually, I had to kick everyone out. Things were getting out of hand and we didn't want the cops showing up. We've already had the cops show up too many times and we haven't even started the season.

Luckily for us, the cops like us. But they like us a little less when they have to keep showing up at our parties. Underage drinking can only be tolerated and ignored for so long.

My phone buzzes in my hand. I know it's a text from Amelia, she's the one keeping me awake right now.

**Smart Girl:** I know you can be easy. I'm just wondering if you're being easy with other girls.

**Me:** Why do you care?

I ask the question again because I really want to know what she's thinking. I wonder what made her ask the question in the first place. I've never really considered whether she's been seeing someone else. I shake that thought out of my head immediately.

**Smart Girl:** I told you already... I don't want to catch anything.

**Me:** What don't you want to catch? Feelings? There's nothing else you can get from me.

I know my message will cause her gorgeous eyes to roll. She hates when I talk about her falling for me. She says it'll never happen. She says she doesn't want a relationship... at least not with me. I should be offended that she feels so strongly about this, but then I have her in my arms whispering my name and I instantly forget everything else she's said. I'm sure she forgets it too, at least in the moment.

It's better for the two of us this way anyway. I don't do relationships and she doesn't want one with me, though that kind of burns a little bit. All the other girls have wanted to marry me, basically, so her not wanting that at all is foreign to me. It's good though. Feelings complicate things and what we have is easy. In a couple of months, she'll be off to law school and I'll be off to an NFL team and that'll be the end of that.

**Smart Girl:** Please... you're more likely to catch feelings for me than I am for you.

**Me:** You're the one asking if you're "the only one."

**Smart Girl:** ...

**Me:** Am I wrong?

**Smart Girl:** Clearly, you're not going to answer my question.

**Me:** Not until you answer me first.

**Smart Girl:** I haven't slept with other guys.

**Me:** Since when?

**Smart Girl:** What do you mean?

**Me:** Who was the last guy you slept with? When did you sleep with him?

I ask the questions both wanting to know the answer and hating what she may say at the same time.

**Smart Girl:** You don't need to know his name. It was before you and I started...

I believe her when she says she hasn't been with anyone else; she has no reason to lie to me. I like knowing that. We've been doing this thing secretly for six months now. Knowing she hasn't seen anyone else makes me proud for some reason. I haven't seen anyone else either, and even though she and the rest of the world may not believe it, it's true.

**Me:** I haven't slept with any other girls.

Damn, I really haven't hooked up with anyone else since March. That's a record.

**Smart Girl:** Somehow, I doubt that.

**Me:** I didn't doubt your response, so why do you doubt mine?

**Smart Girl:** You're Nick Hunter... football player... party aficionado.

**Me:** And you're an intelligent, beautiful woman. Seems like the two of us could have our pick. Somehow, we picked each other.

My message was too much. I know this because I've been waiting ten minutes for her to reply. I know she read the message. I shouldn't have said that at all.

**Me:** I was kidding, by the way.

I tell her, feeling the need to make sure she knows I'm not out here talking about relationships or anything. To make sure she doesn't think there's anything serious behind my words. I know her enough to know that any sign of more than no-strings-attached would have her running for the hills. She wouldn't want to be with me if she thought I felt anything serious for her.

# 4

## AMELIA

The first game of the football season is in four days and the only reason I know is that my sister's already driving me nuts. "We didn't agree to this, you know?" I tell my sister as I lock the door to our apartment and follow her out the door.

"I know, I know. But help a girl out," she begs again, making puppy dog eyes at me. She still gets whatever she wants from Mom and our stepdad when she does that. It's annoying.

We exit the elevator and make our way outside. "We share the car. I have my days and you have yours. We literally picked our classes to match our schedules, which included your practices. Why wasn't this on the calendar?" I'm a planner and this defeats the purpose of a schedule.

My sister continues to walk and I follow behind her. "This was not expected. We didn't have this practice on the calendar. Gisele said we'd be adding practices as needed. We have to be perfect. I'll owe you big time," she says.

I'll hold her to that. "That's the only reason I'm giving you a ride," I tell her.

"You'll have to pick me up too," she adds.

I take quicker steps and catch up to her. "Now you're pushing it. I could've been sleeping."

"You could still be in bed if you just let me borrow the car," she replies.

"I would have, trust me, but I have something to do later." I look back longingly at our apartment where my bed begged me to stay a little longer.

"Something or someone?" she asks. I know she's talking about Nick. I hate when she does that. I haven't seen him in a few days. I basically haven't responded to him since he started talking about us picking each other. Even though he said he was joking, it was too much.

I didn't hate it. I liked the direction the conversation was taking and that's why I had to stop it. Though it's only been a few days without seeing or talking to him and I already miss him. That's a problem too. I shouldn't miss him. I shouldn't feel anything other than lust for him. Real emotions aren't part of the plan. And yet the entire time I was at home this summer, I wished I were at school. So yeah, I think time away from each other is what we need to get our thoughts in order.

Bringing my attention back to my sister, I pin her with a glare. "Don't start with that again. I'll turn around, go back to bed, and you'll be left walking to practice."

"When will you guys finally go public with this?" she presses, because Elia doesn't know when to stop.

I stop in my tracks. Elia looks back when she realizes I'm not keeping up with her. I cross my arms as I stand a few feet away from our car. "Sorry, sorry. I'll stop. I promise," she says, instantly apologizing.

I uncross my arms and walk the rest of the way to the driver side. "So, where am I taking you?" I say after we both get into the car.

"The football stadium," she replies with a devious smile on her face.

I start coughing uncontrollably while my sister throws her bag in the back seat then turns around and puts her seatbelt on.

"What did you have to do later?" she asks.

"I have class," I remind her. She should know the schedule. It's only the second week of classes but I can already see that this will be one of the hardest courses I've ever taken. I'd love to drop it but I need it so I can boost my transcript. I need to stand out when I start applying for law schools in the spring if I want to get into a good one.

"Is it one of the terrible ones?" she asks.

I nod. These classes question my career choice. The exams will only get worse from here.

"Well, I'll call you when I'm done with practice so you can pick me up when you finish class. I think this will take about the same time your class will take you," she says.

"You could always use Lyft, you know?" It's not like having a car is the only way to get around.

She gasps. "And ride with a stranger? Absolutely not!"

I laugh at her terror then turn on the car and pull out of the parking lot. "That's just such a weird fear to have in this day and age."

"I guess I'm the only one who cares about being kidnapped," she bites back.

"You wouldn't be." At least, I haven't heard any stories of people being kidnapped by their drivers. Then again, I've never looked into it, so there could be a few.

"You don't know that," she argues.

I don't bother arguing with her. I'm too tired to try and fight with Elia about something that's not going to change. Instead, I turn on the radio and begin searching for a song to wake me up. "Just text me when you're done," I tell her as I stop changing the station when I recognize a rock song I like.

"You're the best," she says and I turn briefly in her direction to see her smile.

I fix my eyes on the road ahead and, just as the song is about to get to my favorite part, a different song comes on. "Are you kidding me?!" I say when I realize Elia is the one responsible for the interruption.

"Passenger gets radio, that's always been the rule!" she says, shrugging, then continues searching for a song that'll satisfy her.

"We also made rules about who gets the car and when. We're breaking that one today, so the least you can do is let me listen to music!" I can't believe I'm up at 6 am for this.

"I would if you listened to things I enjoyed. I don't know how you can listen to this stuff. It's so dark," she replies and I can imagine the judgment on her face.

"Well, your music is too happy and light," I reply. Polar opposites, I tell you. Whenever we ride together, one of us is always miserable with the other's music choices.

"Kind of like me," she says as she lands on a song she approves of. I watch her lean back on her chair and close her eyes from the corner of mine. Great, she gets to nap while I have to be her chauffeur. I'm glad she woke me up for this.

JUST AS THE ROCK SONG I CHOSE COMES TO AN END, I ARRIVE AT THE parking lot of the stadium. Luckily for me, Elia fell asleep right away, so I didn't have to endure her terrible taste in music for more than two songs. I envy how she can just fall asleep in a matter of seconds.

I park the car in the lot and then do the most obnoxious thing Elia would do if she were me. "Elia!" I scream her name so loud that it startles her.

She gets up from the seat as if it were on fire and hits her head on the rooftop. "What?!" she shouts back, looking around to see if something is wrong.

"Nothing, we're here," I tell her, laughing.

"I hate you," she replies, her hand caressing the top of her head.

I smile at her. "I'm your favorite sister."

"You're my only sister," she replies through gritted teeth.

"Same difference. You're here. Get out of my car!" I tell her.

"Our car," she corrects.

"Whatever," I tell her.

"Incoming," she says as she gets out of the car.

"What?" I ask, but then a tap on my window gets my attention.


## NICK


I DON'T BELIEVE WHAT I'M SEEING UNTIL ELIA GETS OUT OF THE CAR. Yup. That's definitely Amelia parked in the lot. Ignoring what my teammates are saying next to me, I walk straight toward her without giving it a second thought.

Elia gets out of the car and I hear her say incoming just as I tap on Amelia's window.

Amelia turns to look at me and I can see the surprise in her eyes as she sees me. I wait for her to roll down her window or open the door, but when she does neither, I walk around and get into the seat Elia vacated.

"Hi," I tell her, closing the door.

"What-what are—" she starts, clearly at a loss for words.

"What am I doing here, you ask?" I finish her sentence for her.

She nods.

I look down and take in her outfit. Her hair is in a bun on top of her head. She's wearing sweatpants with vans and a sweater. She looks cute. Her outfit hides the curves I've gotten the chance to explore intimately though. "I've got practice," I tell her when I finally stop checking her out. "I've got a game on Saturday," I add. I stop myself from extending an invitation, knowing I'm on thin ice.

"Oh..." she says and I can see her cheeks redden. Is she nervous? She has been ignoring me, so I wouldn't be surprised that having me in her car right now is surprising.

"Yeah, this is my workplace," I add with a smile on my face. Seeing her today was definitely unexpected, but I'm not mad about it. I've missed her.

She nods again. She does that a lot. "What are you doing in my car?" she asks then looks around as if searching to see if anyone can see us.

My guys are no longer lingering in the parking lot. They're likely in the locker room dropping off their things and getting ready for practice. We have our first game this coming weekend. This game will tell us how we're doing. After replacing so many guys, I wouldn't be shocked if we lost.

I want us to win though. I'm playing for my future right now. Although the scrimmages and practices have been good, Saturday we'll know how the team does under the pressure of a real opponent.

"What am I doing in your car?" I repeat her question. "Well, since you came to see me I didn't want to be rude," I tell her, knowing that'll get a reaction out of her.

Her mouth opens and closes before she speaks. "I did not come here to see you."

"Are you sure about that? You did ask me if I were seeing other girls, maybe this is your way of checking up on me... since you've been ignoring me?" I know exactly what to say to get her to look at me with that fire in her eyes that I like so much. I've missed that. She's ignored me for way too long, three days to be exact, and I'm about to show her what she's been missing.

"I haven't been ignoring you," she argues. Yeah, right.

I pin her with a look. Then opt for a different strategy. "I can see I was wrong now that you came to see me." Somehow I decide pressing the same buttons that got her to ignore me in the first place is a good idea.

"I came to drop off my sister, not to see you," she bites back and I smile again.

"So, I'm right, then. You have been ignoring me," I tell her, feeling like law could be a nice backup career for me.

She sighs loudly and I know that means she's run out of arguments. I know her enough to know when she's given up. "I have been busy."

"Me too," I tell her.

"What have you been busy doing?" she fires back so quickly that it actually makes me laugh.

"Being ignored by you," I reply then wink at her.

"You're starting to sound like someone who's catching feelings," she says, mocking my earlier words.

"Nah, not catching feelings. More like missing those late nights," I reply, biting my lip as I fix my eyes on hers. I haven't felt those on mine in too long.

Her cheeks redden. "Right."

"Are we having one of those soon or should I go searching elsewhere?" I ask and the moment the words leave my mouth I wish I could take them back. I was trying to sound casual. To dispel any ideas that there's more to this than what we originally agreed on, but I think I took it way too far.

Nope, I don't think, I know. I can see it in her eyes. Her expression. "If it's so easy to

replace me, then by all means, get it elsewhere. Just let me know once you do." There's no humor in the tone of her voice, just annoyance.

"Why?" I ask.

"Because then we're done."

"Are you saying we're something? We have to be something before we can be done," I tell her, trying to twist her words in my favor yet again. Apparently, I don't learn.

# 5

## AMELIA

He's exasperating. Frustrating. He's everything I've never needed and yet somehow I find myself wanting. Ignoring him hasn't changed anything. And here he is teasing me, trying to rile me up, and it's working. He knows which buttons to press. He knows me better than I'd like.

"We're less than friends," I tell him, trying not to give him a label he can run with.

He clutches his chest. "Ouch. Way to care about my feelings."

"We said no feelings," I remind him.

He smiles. "I know. I'm just kidding. You gotta relax a little. I can think of a few ways to help if you want," he finishes.

I smack him on the arm. "Stop it!" I look around, wondering if there's a chance someone else may see us. Some of the other football players. The cheerleaders. I wouldn't want them to get the wrong impression or, I guess, the right one? "Don't you have practice?"

"As a matter of fact, I do," he says, finally agreeing with me on something. He opens the door then turns to me. "What kind of food would you like for dinner tonight?"

"Food?" I ask.

"If you're not ignoring me, I'd like to come over tonight. I'll even feed you. I think after practice and class I'll be in desperate need of a massage too."

I can't believe how cocky he is. I've never given him a massage. "Who said I would give you a massage?" I ask, trying to sound outraged at the insinuation but finding myself not entirely opposed to it.

His boyish smile returns and I try so hard to not smile in return. "I never thought you would but figured if I add a crazy third request, then you'd agree to the first two. So, what kind of food would you like to eat?"

"Surprise me," I tell him, surprising myself with my response.

He smiles. "Sounds good to me."

"Hey Hunter, you're going to be late!" someone yells and I feel like I just got caught doing something wrong, which I am. My mother would agree.

"I'm coming!" Nick shouts. "I'll see you later, babe," he says, closing my door and walking away before I have a chance to fight with him about calling me that.

---

I WALK OUT OF CLASS AND INSTANTLY RECEIVE A MESSAGE FROM ELIA asking me to pick her up. My heart picks up speed as I think about the possibility of running into Nick again.

I've thought about that moment since it happened this morning, it actually distracted me from paying attention to the professor's lecture in class today.

It's crazy that the thought of seeing him throws me off. I see him all the time but this time was more jarring. Perhaps because I had been ignoring him but also maybe because I barely see him out in the world. Usually, it's just in my house.

**Me:** On my way. Make sure you're outside in five minutes.

**Elia:** I'll try.

**Me:** I'll leave you if you're not out in time.

**Elia:** Why do you have to be so mean? I figured you'd be happy since you got to see him.

I don't even bother to respond to her message but instead drive over to the stadium and pray the entire time that I don't run into him again. At least not in his territory.

I arrive there at the five-minute mark and text Elia right away. When three more minutes pass and she doesn't respond, I give her a call.

Her phone rings and rings but she doesn't answer. I'm about to leave her a voicemail telling her I'm leaving her behind when the passenger door to my car swings open, scaring me. "It's just me, calm down!" Elia says, tossing her bag in the back and getting in.

"I was about to leave you," I tell her when I finally catch my breath.

Elia does her signature eye roll. "Do you have another class?" she asks.

I shake my head.

"Then what's the rush?" she questions.

I don't answer but instead pull out of the parking lot.

"Ahh, you don't want to see him again," Elia says interpreting my silence. "How come? Trouble in paradise?" She's never going to let this go.

"There is no paradise," I tell her.

"What's going on? You know you can talk to me," she says as she starts messing with the radio again.

I don't want to talk about it to anyone but especially to her. I know Mom warned us and I've used the warning plenty of times against my own sister to know that what I'm doing is wrong. "I'm good."

37

"Did you find out if he's sleeping with other girls?" she asks. That's the question that started this whole awkward mess in the first place. The reason I've been avoiding him. "I knew it!" she exclaims when I don't answer her question again.

"He's not sleeping with anyone else," I tell her defensively. I hate that I feel like I have to defend him but I do it anyway.

"What?" I ask when I feel her still watching me.

"You're telling me that Nick Hunter, *the* Nick Hunter, is only with you?" she asks.

I'm starting to become frustrated. "Why is that so hard to believe?"

"I don't know. Maybe because his reputation precedes him. He's not a one-woman type of man," she responds, changing the station.

"Well, he's not sleeping with anyone else," I tell her.

"And you believe him?" If she weren't my sister, I wouldn't bother to answer her question. Instead, I'd walk away. But part of having a sister is listening to them say the things you don't want to hear.

I think about everything before I give her a response. I believe him because it just feels right but there's got to be a logical explanation too. "Well, for someone who is a player, I don't think he has a reason to lie to me. He knows we're not in a relationship. I never said he couldn't be with anyone else. I don't think he has an interest in lying."

"Okay," Elia says, settling on a station and increasing the volume. That was easy, too easy. I don't know if she believes me or if she's over this conversation.

"Is that all?" I ask.

I glance briefly in her direction to find her nodding. "I feel like I have to question his motives and whatnot because he's an athlete and you know what Mom said about them," my sister reminds me.

"Yeah, I know," I tell her.

"But he's not half bad."

"You just said he's known for being a playboy!" I exclaim. She can't change her mind about him so quickly. Not after questioning him a minute ago.

Elia leans back on her chair and I see her shrug from the corner of my eye. "Maybe it's that seeing him at our place is making me warm up to him. Maybe we should go to a party and see him in his natural habitat so I can go back to disliking him again."

A party is where I met him in person. A party was when I became attracted to him. I'm not sure I want to be at a party where he is ever again. Being at the parking lot of the stadium is about as close to his territory as I want to get. "Let's not do that," I tell her.

"Suit yourself, but if he keeps coming around and making jokes, I may start to think he's a good guy," she responds.

Well, I'm sure him coming over tonight and bringing food will definitely not help.

# 6

## NICK

"So, am I living up to your standards?" Lincoln asks as we walk out of the locker room.

I nod. "So far, so good, rookie," I tell him. He's been playing very well so far. "The true test is on the field Saturday," I remind him.

"Then you'll finally call a truce and let me live my life?" He asks jokingly.

I shrug. "Maybe. I'm still salty that you refuse to live in the house with the rest of us."

"No way I'm choosing to live with a bunch of dudes instead of my girlfriend," he tells me. "I heard your brother basically moved in with his girl the last year too," he adds, trying to make his case.

"My brother earned it though. He lived in that house for the first three years and the beginning of the fourth. You've never even spent the night. You know you have a room there, right?" I ask, but I'm not as bothered by it anymore; now I just enjoy bothering him.

"I'm sure you guys make good use of it," he says, patting me on the shoulder.

"All my dirty laundry is there," I tell him, laughing, as we reach the lot.

Lincoln shakes his head. "Joke's on you... I'm never going to need it. You can use it to store whatever you want," he says.

"I'm really trying to not dislike you," I tell him.

"You have no reason to other than the—"

"Fact that you're breaking tradition while you're supposed to be leading this team?" I finish for him. I mean, I'm the captain, but he's the quarterback. That position always comes with a leadership role, even if it isn't necessarily earned.

We reach the exit door then step outside and into the parking lot. "Here's the deal. I'll try to go to some of the parties. I won't sleep there though. But I'll try to come around more often."

"You can bring your girl too if you'd like," I tell him. I'm curious as to what she's like, this guy seems to be head over heels for her.

He extends his hand to me and I shake it, sealing our new deal. "I'll let her know. Now, will you stop hating me?"

"I never hated you," I reply.

He looks at me skeptically.

"Okay fine, I did in the beginning. But that's old news now!" I add, throwing my hand over his shoulder. "Speaking of, can I get a ride home?" I ask. "One of the new guys gave me a ride here because I wanted to try and sleep a little bit on the way here."

He laughs. "You're unbelievable."

"We're friends now!" I tell him. "This is a perk of friendship."

"You're saying I'm rewarded by becoming your personal driver?" he says.

"At least we don't haze people here," I tell him.

The smile leaves his face instantly. "Are you headed to the Football House?" he asks. His voice sounds tense, and the way he ignored my remark about hazing shows me there's more there than meets the eye. I don't bother asking though, we officially buried the hatchet seconds ago, we're not about to start telling each other our secrets.

"Yes, sir!" I reply proudly. Like that House is the greatest thing to ever exist. Maybe it is. To me, it was an instant family when I got to campus. It's brotherhood. I love it there, even though it smells and is dirtier than it should be, which reminds me, I really need to get the guys to start cleaning up after themselves. I want to punch myself in the face after thinking about cleaning. Who am I turning into? I swear I've got Jesse, Colton, and Chase all living in my head now.

WE WALK THE REST OF THE WAY TO LINCOLN'S JEEP. WHEN HE DOESN'T turn on the radio, I decide I should at least try and get to know him better. "So, what's your story?" I ask the moment we're on the road. He looks at me skeptically, wondering why I'm asking him this question, so I explain. "We have to be more connected than ever now that games are starting. Me and the last quarterback were brothers, so we had a connection that took years to build. You and I have to do the quick version," I joke.

"And for that I have to tell you my story?" he says, looking at me briefly.

"All I know is you're a great quarterback—"

Lincoln interrupts me. "Great, you say?"

I roll my eyes. "Yeah, yeah. At least that's what they said about you before you joined. We'll see what we think after the game."

"I know I know. This week is the true test," he says, repeating what I've been telling all the guys in the locker room the last couple days.

"So, are you going to tell me about you or are we going to sit here in silence until you drop me off?" I ask, returning to the original question.

"What do you want to know?" He asks, and I think about what kind of questions he may answer. He doesn't seem like an over sharer. I mean, I've known him for a couple months now and barely know a thing about him—except he has a girlfriend he lives with.

I guess I'll have to play twenty questions. "Do you have any siblings?"

"I have a little brother," he says. "Ethan," he adds, and I can hear the pride in his voice.

"That's awesome!" I exclaim.

"Yeah, he's pretty cool."

"Little brothers are the best," I tell him. I think Colton and Kaitlyn would disagree but they're not here to say anything.

He shakes his head. "I assume you're the little brother?"

"Of course," I reply jokingly but also very seriously. "How long have you been with your girlfriend?" I ask. She's the one person he's mentioned since he's been here and we haven't met her yet.

"Almost a year," he tells me.

"That's not a long time," I tell him. The guys and I thought he'd been with her his whole life. I mean, why else would he ditch us, right?

"Feels like a lifetime," he responds but he doesn't say it in the 'it feels so long I'm tired of this crap' way. Instead, he says it like he's happy about it. Like he wouldn't want it any other way.

"Really?" I ask. The smile on his face reminds me of all the guys who ended up in long-term relationships. Zack, Colton, and Jesse looked just as happy as Lincoln does right now.

"Yeah. I think once you find someone you really want to be with you just feel things differently," he replies. He sounds like a love-sick puppy and it makes me want to throw up a little bit, I'm not going to lie. He looks at the look of disgust on my face. "You asked! How are you going to make that face when you're the one who asked?!" he exclaims, and this time it's my turn to laugh.

"Sorry, I thought I was keeping my reaction internal," I tell him.

He shakes his head. "If that's you keeping your reaction to yourself, I can't imagine you actually trying," he starts "It'll make sense to you eventually," he adds, like he's all-knowing wise or something. This kid is younger than I am.

"What will?" I ask, curious to see specifically what he's referring to.

"Wanting to be with someone," he replies.

I know what he means by that, but I go for an answer that'll frustrate him. "I love being with many women," I tell him.

He sighs loudly. "I mean only one. No one else. Being completely satisfied with just the one person."

Who is this guy? "You sound like the main character of one of those chick flicks." Not realistic at all. We round the corner to the Football House and I immediately start making a mental checklist of the things I need to get done before I can finally go over to Amelia's tonight.

"It's not like that at all. I mean, it's not all butterflies and rainbows," Lincoln says. I thought this conversation was over.

"And yet you stay?" If it's not good, why bother, I wonder.

"The good times always outweigh. I couldn't imagine being anywhere else." Yeah, this conversation is way more than I bargained for. That's what I get for not keeping my mouth shut.

# 7

AMELIA

I wake up from my nap to the sound of my phone ringing. Feeling hazy, I open my eyes and begin searching for it. Finding it under my pillow, I prepare myself for the brightness that'll hit me the moment I flip it over. When I do, it's not the brightness that has the largest impact; instead, it's the name I have for Nick on my screen that does the damage.

I think about letting it go to voicemail but I can't help picking it up. "Hello," I respond, sounding groggy. I figured I'd take a nap after coming back from class but it feels like I slept for way too many hours.

"Did you just wake up?" he asks. We don't really talk on the phone, so I'm not used to the richness of his voice. I nod but then realize he can't see me. "Did you just nod?" he asks.

"How did you—" I look around the room to make sure he didn't sneak in here, though that's a ridiculous thought because I'd hear his voice somewhere other than my ear.

"I know you, Amelia," he says, his words waking me right up.

"Doubt it," I tell him, feeling like I don't want to give him any concessions.

"Of course, the first thing you do after waking up is argue with me," he says.

"You called me, what do you want?" I ask, lying back down.

He chuckles and I feel that in every part of my body. I could get used to that sound. I kind of already have. "I'm outside," he says, and those words send goosebumps down my back. I move the phone from my ear and look at the time. "It's only 7 pm, what are you doing here now?" I ask. This is a lot earlier than it usually is when he comes over.

"We didn't agree on a time... so I figured food would be good now. It is dinner time and I'm hungry." he replies.

I get up from my bed and start searching for my shoes. "You should've given me a heads up. Told me that you were on your way," I tell him, fumbling around in the dark.

"All good, I'm just hanging out in the living room with your sister," he replies nonchalantly.

"You're what?!" I shout, dropping the phone onto the floor.

I grab my phone from the floor at the same time my sister yells. "I'm hungry, come out here already! We let you sleep long enough." They let me sleep long enough? How long has he been here?

Minutes later, I walk out of my room fully dressed to find my sister and Nick sitting on the couch with Chinese food laid out on the coffee table. They don't even notice that I'm there as they chat away about which movie to choose for tonight. Who said we were watching a movie?

They look so normal. Like we do this all the time. Like this is just another night of my sister, my—Nick, and me hanging out. It's not normal. Not even a little bit.

"This is weird," I tell them, interrupting their conversation.

Nick looks at me and just smiles. I try really hard not to smile back. "Why? He's here all the time anyway, so we may as well get to know each other," Elia replies. I want to kick her but I refrain because it won't make a difference. We already argued today and I don't want to do it again.

"You don't need to be friends with him," I tell her.

"Oh babe, you don't have to be jealous," Nick cuts in and I grab the nearest pillow.

I aim the pillow in his direction. "Stop!" I yell, warning him.

He laughs, a belly laugh, and my sister joins him. And despite how much I want this to not be a thing, it makes me laugh too. "Are you going to just stand there threatening me with a pillow or are you going to sit here and eat with us?" Nick asks, tapping the couch cushion next to him.

I shake my head at him. "You're annoying," I tell him then walk around and sit on the other side of him. Not the one he pointed to because I don't have to follow his instructions. But still next to him because I want to be.

"You guys are too much," my sister says, and I pin her with a look that I hope translates to 'cut it out'.

"Alright, let's eat. Nick brought Chinese food from your favorite spot," Elia says, getting the message.

Nick smirks. "Look at me being great and surprising you by figuring out your favorite place to eat without you telling me. I guess I do always know what you want," he says, his words laced with double meaning.

"Shut up," I tell him, grabbing one of the containers with rice and chicken. Picking up a fork, I start stuffing my face. If we're going to do this awkward movie with my sister, then I'm at least going to enjoy the food—it is from my favorite place after all.


NICK


SHE SITS THERE EATING HER FOOD AND LOOKING BACK AND FORTH between her sister and me as we try and have a conversation. I know it's weird for her that I'm here hanging out with them instead of just going straight to her room. I want to do that too, trust me. Her room is where I'll end up at the end of the night, but I'm more than a piece of meat. And for some reason, this is the first time in my life I've wanted other people to know that. I've wanted a girl to know that.

"So, what game are you playing here?" Elia asks with her fork midair as she looks at me.

"What do you mean?" I ask.

"Elia, cut it out," Amelia says through gritted teeth. Oh, now I definitely want to know more.

"No, let her speak. I'm intrigued," I tell her, picking up my own container of food and a fork and start eating. Man, I am starving.

"Well, you and my sister have been doing your thing for almost six months now," she says, pointing at us with her fork.

"It's been that long? I hadn't noticed," Amelia says, trying to sound cool.

I can tell you the exact date we started doing this thing, so I've noticed. I'm sure she has too. "Yup. And?" I ask, taking a bite of the chicken.

"And now you're bringing food and hanging out with us," she says, finally bringing her fork to her mouth.

"This is the first time I've done that," I say, agreeing with her.

"And the last," Amelia mutters under her breath.

I bring my hand to her knee and wait for Elia to speak again. "Are you guys dating?" she asks and I feel Amelia tense up.

Before she has a chance to answer, I speak up. "Not really," I tell her, because it's true. We aren't dating. "But it doesn't hurt to get to know each other better. First steps and all, you know," I joke.

"Very funny," Amelia says, poking me on the side. "Could you stop, Elia? I can make things really bad for you," Amelia threatens her twin and I laugh at their exchange.

"Fine," Elia says. "I can feel the awkwardness in the room, so I'll go ahead and start this movie before this gets even weirder."

"Thank you!" Amelia replies, and I remove my hand from her knee and go back to eating my food. I'm ready for an interesting night with the Kings.

# 8

## AMELIA

The movie ends and just as quickly, I get up from the couch and take the empty containers to the kitchen. I couldn't wait to get out of there with my sister making eyes at me from her end of the couch. I should've put a stop to this the moment it started. Honestly, it should've never started.

"Maybe next time we can do a game night?" I hear Nick say as I step back into the living room.

"There will not be a next time," I reply, a little more rudely than intended.

I watch as the smile on his face is replaced by confusion, then there's just a blank expression on his face. Nick gets up from the couch then, and I'm half ready for him to follow me into my room when instead he turns to my sister. "Thanks for having me," he says to her. Then, he walks out the door and doesn't turn back. Did he just leave?

"Way to hurt his feelings," Elia says, getting up and heading to her own room. I stand there in the living room stunned. I have no idea what just happened but clearly it wasn't good.

I just pissed off my sister and Nick at the same time.

AFTER A FEW MINUTES OF MULLING OVER WHAT JUST HAPPENED, I HEAD over to my room. I instantly go for my phone. There are no new messages. Well, there are but not from the person I want there to be. I'm disappointed but not surprised. He left here without even saying goodbye to me.

"Ugh!" I scream into my pillow because I feel frustrated. I didn't mean to be rude to him but I was uncomfortable by how normal it all felt. It seemed like a casual hangout between my sister, boyfriend, and me. But I don't have a boyfriend. That's not what Nick is and I couldn't allow him or my sister to think this could happen again. I can't let myself think that. That's not part of the plan. My plan.

**Me:** Are you mad?

I ask, sending a text message after debating it for all of five minutes. I shouldn't have sent it but I do it anyway because I want to make whatever I ruined better. Because my night ended a lot differently than I expected. And I won't be able to get any sleep tonight until it's resolved.

I wait and wait for him to respond and, when he doesn't, I decide I need to go for a run. Putting on some sweatpants and running shoes, I close the door to my apartment and walk outside. It's a little after 10 pm right now, and while I maybe shouldn't go for a run this late, I need to. I need to distract my mind because, otherwise, I'll be stuck thinking about Nick. Karma, right? I did ignore his message for three days and he's ignored mine for less than an hour and here I am driving myself crazy. See, this is exactly why I need to be running right now.

. . .

I RUN AROUND THE SAME FEW BLOCKS OVER AND OVER AGAIN. I RUN until I can't feel my legs and when I think about Nick, I run some more. Honestly, maybe this is the best thing for both of us, to end this before anyone gets hurt.

# 9

NICK

I t's been four days since I talked to Amelia. The only message
she sent me on Tuesday night still burning a hole in my pocket.
But I couldn't give in. Not until I had proven a point, what the
point was I don't remember.

We won today. Still, it was hard to focus on my first game because
my mind was too busy thinking about her. It's a miracle we didn't get
our asses handed to us today. The first win of the season under our
belts and somehow that doesn't put me in a better mood.

"The life of the party is back!" one of the new guys shouts the
moment I walk through the doors of the Football House.

"You guys are throwing a party?" I ask, though I really shouldn't
because it's evident. This is what we do after we win a home game.

I notice that they've put all the furniture away already. It's only
been a couple hours since the game ended and yet people are
packing every inch of the house. I stretch, feeling my body hurt from
the hits I took out on the field today.

The newbie smiles. I really should learn his name but right now I can't be bothered. "Yeah, don't you love it?" he asks with a grin on his face. He reminds me of me which, at any other time, would've been hilarious, but right now just pisses me off.

"Didn't bother to ask if you could?" I ask him loudly so that he can hear me over the music.

He shrugs. He's confused and I understand it. "Isn't this what we always do?" he says. "We can send everyone home if you want," he says, scratching the back of his neck trying to figure out how to make sure I'm not angry with him.

I put on a smile because I feel bad that I'm taking out my bad mood on him. He's right. This is what we do. We don't need permission because it's tradition. "I'm just kidding! Let's get this party started!!" I tell him. Rodriguez, the kicker who replaced Jesse when his workload prevented him from continuing to play with us, walks by at that very moment with a tray of shots in hand. "Rodriguez," I call him over.

"Yes?" he replies.

"Give me one of those," I tell him, taking one of the shots. I throw it and taste the tequila as it makes its way down, not bad. "I'll take another one," I tell him and throw that one back too.

I wasn't really in the mood to party but at least this will distract me from everything else.

---

"SHOT SHOT SHOT SHOT SHOT, EVERYBODY!" WHY IS IT THAT WHEN people are drinking, this song always comes on and gets people to drink even more? We hear the song and lose our collective minds.

I've been drinking for the last two hours and I can't for the life of me remember how many shots and beers I've had. All I know is I can barely make out the faces of the people right in front of me. The other thing I know is I don't want to stop.

I take another shot then grab another from the person in front of me. He's wearing a jersey with the number 4 displayed on the back.

Who wears a jersey to a party? Oh wait, I say, looking down and realizing I have one on. I guess I do. "That wasn't yours," the guy says, turning around.

"Want me to give it back to you?" I ask, smiling at him, knowing it'll likely piss him off.

He scowls and I laugh. "You think this is a joke?" he asks.

Why do people always ask me that? "I think you're a joke," I tell him, patting him on the shoulder. I turn around and take the shot. Just as I'm about to hand the glass to one of the newbies, I feel someone pull at my shirt. The moment I turn back around, the same guy's fist hits me straight in the face.

I sober up instantly, at least I think I do. I look at him dead in the eyes because I want him to see what's coming. The moment realization hits him, I take him down. Down like I'm a defensive tackle and he's the guy standing between me and the quarterback. If only my body didn't hurt so much already, I could do some real damage.

I hear the people shouting behind me but I don't focus on it. I'm too busy dodging punches and throwing some of my own to care about what they're saying.

"Stop!" I hear someone scream.

More screams, some chants, and then arms try to pry me away from him. I can tell I'm not sober when, in the middle of the fight, I start to think about how pissed Colton would be if he showed up right now. Just as I start imagining the disappointed look on his face, the guy lands another punch on mine, knocking me back.

I get mad at myself, then. If I had been paying attention to the task at hand, I could've avoided the bruise that hit will likely leave behind.

Punching him a few times, I start to get into a rhythm. I'm about to attack again when I'm pulled back, but this time I can't manage to fight them off. When I get a look at who's pulling me, I realize it's one of the o-linemen. No one can really get through them and so I stop my futile attempt to get him to let me go. Those guys are like walls. I'd have a better chance pulling a car off me. Okay, maybe that's an exaggeration.

I watch a few of my teammates pick up jersey guy from the floor. I don't know what it is about the hockey team not listening. "We told you guys you weren't welcome here," I tell him, my blood boiling.

"You didn't tell me shit," he spits back, and I recognize the guy as the same guy I saw Chase almost tear to pieces at the cafeteria last year. I still wonder what he said that day to piss off Boulder.

"Well, I hope you got the message now," I tell him, seeing the blood running down his face and tasting my own on my lips.

The guy is escorted out of the house and I decide the party's over, at least for me. Heading to my room, I walk through the kitchen and out the back door. I linger when I reach the yard and see the fire pit and the chairs where the guys and their girls would usually be. I miss seeing them all sitting out here having their bon fires. I missed it more when they were all single, but at least having girlfriends made them happy, and they still showed up to the party, even if they never came inside.

The thought of what it'd be like to join them with my own girl-friend briefly crosses my mind before I shake it off. No point in thinking about things that will never happen.

I walk past all that and into the room that was previously occu-pied by my brother. I walk straight toward the bed, taking off my shoes and jersey in the process. Then, I grab my phone from the left pocket of my jeans before shedding the pants too.

I unlock it and head straight to the message that's been on my mind for days. The one from Smart Girl.

# 10

## NICK

I think about it a million times over before I decide to finally respond. I'm just hopeful I'm sober enough to not sound like an idiot. I wonder if she'll be even more mad at me for having ignored her. She ignored me, so this just makes us even.

**Me:** I'm mad at the guy who made me bleed.

**Smart Girl:** I'm sorry, what? A guy made you bleed? What happened?

I probably shouldn't have started with that, but I knew it would get me a response.

**Me:** Just a little fight.

**Smart Girl:** And you're bleeding?

**Me:** Only a little.

**Smart Girl:** Why?

**Me:** Why am I bleeding?

**Smart Girl:** Why did you get into a fight?

**Me:** The guy punched me, so I hit him back.

Okay, that wasn't the full story. Some would say I instigated it by stealing his drink, but it's my house. My alcohol. I'm sure the hockey idiot didn't bring the alcohol to our house himself. My house, my rules. I also already told him that he wasn't welcome here. Maybe not him directly but the entire hockey team. Can't they just throw their own parties? Why do they have to crash ours?

I think about why I'm telling Amelia this. I don't want her to think I'm a meathead, an idiot, but I do want to see if she worries about me. If she cares enough to ask me more questions. To ask me if I'm okay. After the last few days, I just want a sign that I mean something to her. Even if only a little.

I doubt she'll care though. We're not even friends, she made that clear to me on Tuesday. So why did I pick a fight and why do I want her to know about it?

**Smart Girl:** Are you okay?

**Me:** Doesn't matter.

**Smart Girl:** What do you mean?

**Me:** We don't have to talk about these things. It's not the kind of relationship we have.

**Smart Girl:** Stop that. Where are you right now? Are you still bleeding? Are you okay? Is anyone with you?

**Me:** I'm going to bed.

My phone buzzes a couple of times, but I can't get my eyes to open. I'm too tired. Instead, I get more and more comfortable in my bed and go to sleep.

---

I HEAR BANGING ON MY DOOR. I OPEN MY EYES, FEELING MY BLOOD START to boil. Why would someone be knocking at my door right now?

The banging continues and I stand up. I make my way toward the door, stumbling a little. Definitely still drunk, I see.

"What?!" I scream, throwing the door open. I'm surprised when I see Amelia's eyes looking up at me slightly frightened. "I'm so sorry, I didn't mean to yell... well I did, but I didn't mean to yell at you."

"It's okay," she tells me. What is she doing here?

Wait, why am I asking that question inside of my head? "What are you doing here?" I ask out loud.

I take in her appearance. She's wearing jeans and an oversized hoodie. Her hair is up in that messy bun I love. "I wanted to make sure you were okay," she says, her words barely a whisper.

"Really?" I ask, hope spreading through me.

"I'm not heartless. From what I gathered from your texts you got into a fight, clearly you were bleeding," she says, her hand reaching toward me. She touches the spot on my face where I assume the blood is now dry and I flinch. He must've gotten a good hit. "And then you just said you were going to bed. I wanted to make sure you were okay. Not going to bed with a concussion and all."

"He didn't hit me that hard," I joke.

"Still, I wanted to see for myself that you were good," she says, and I can see the worry in her eyes.

I bring my hand to her cheek. "How did you know I was home?"

"You said you were going to bed. I assumed you'd sleep on your own. I hoped I was right." This brings flashbacks of our conversation about sleeping with other people. Hopefully, this helps her believe me if she didn't.

"Well, you were. Here I am," I tell her. "Do you want to come in?" I ask.

She looks behind her suddenly like she just realized where she was. I know she's trying to make sure no one else knows she's here. I wish she didn't care about who sees us together. "If you're ashamed of anyone seeing you with me, you can just leave," I tell her, dropping my hand and stepping back.

"Wait," she says, and I stop in my tracks. When did I get so dramatic? "I didn't know where your room was."

I look at her, confused. "You seem to have found it without trouble," I tell her.

"I had to ask one of your teammates where you were," she says, and I instantly get what that

means. The girl who fears anyone thinking there's something between us came searching for me. In the moment, she didn't care who saw her or what they thought about us.

"Really? You asked someone for me?" I ask in disbelief. "And you weren't ashamed of even saying my name?"

"I was more ashamed of the clothes I was wearing when I walked through the raging party," she says with a smile.

I take her appearance in once more. "You look better than all the girls in there," I tell her.

She shakes her head and I laugh.

"So, do you want to come in and check out where I live?"

She sighs. "Sure. Why not?"

Extending my hand to her, I lead her inside of the room. There isn't much in here. Just a bed and drawer to hold my things. Everything's neatly organized. I think I felt bad about making this place messy when my brother kept it so pristine. It's a nice change from the chaos in the house, so I kept it up.

"So this is where I live," I tell her.

"What happened?" She asks, instantly sitting down on my bed

and looking like she belongs there. I don't mind that sight.

I sit down next to her. "What do you mean?"

"Why did you get into a fight?" she asks, cutting straight to the chase. I thought she was going to ask me why I've been ignoring her but I guess the answer to that one is pretty obvious.

"The guy punched me first," I tell her the same thing I think I told her earlier.

She turns to face me and I follow her lead. "He didn't punch you for no reason," she says knowingly.

I smile. "I stole his shot."

"His shot?"

"Yeah. He had a drink in his hand. The shot song was playing and I didn't have one. So I took his and apparently that pissed him off," I tell her, laughing.

She gives me a serious look. "That's not funny."

"He thought the same thing when I laughed after he called me out on it. Still, he hit me first, so technically I acted in self-defense."

"You're an idiot," she says, shaking her head.

"Ouch, don't spare my feelings," I tell her.

"You don't have any," she replies.

I look at her for a beat too long. "That's what you keep telling yourself."

"Do you have alcohol?" she asks, ignoring my statement.

"My shot story made you want to drink?" I ask her, surprised.

She shakes her head. "No. I meant rubbing alcohol so we can clean the blood and make sure nothing gets infected."

"You think I might be infected?" I ask, standing up and heading over to the bathroom to quickly retrieve the alcohol.

"I don't know! But better careful than sorry. I can't believe you just fought over a shot," she shouts.

I find the rubbing alcohol in the medicine cabinet. "I can't believe you haven't said anything about the fact that I'm just standing here in my underwear!" I say, changing the conversation.

"It's not like I haven't seen it before," she replies, chuckling, and that makes me smile.

# 11

## AMELIA

Even though I have seen him before it doesn't make him any less of a sight to behold. The way his muscles constrict with each step he takes. The confidence he exudes. Those things I could see every day and never get used to. "You're checking me out an awful lot for a person who seems unbothered by my naked state," he says, catching me. It's not my fault that I hadn't seen or talked to him in four days, I guess it's partially my fault.

I look up and meet his eyes. "You're not naked."

"I can change that if you want," he replies.

"Keep the remainder of your clothes on and give me the rubbing alcohol so I can clean up the blood," I say, trying to sound serious and unaffected.

"I thought we didn't do this," he says, pointing back and forth between the two of us. His words remind me of my earlier ones.

I take the rubbing alcohol from his hand. "Do you have a paper towel?" I ask.

"Just take the jersey. There's blood already on that too. Not sure if it's mine or his though, so just don't touch the bloody parts," he replies and I take a deep calming breath.

Tonight is not going the way I thought it would. It's been a roller-coaster the last few days. I've been running every night whenever I'm not doing homework or in class. I had just gotten back to the house after what are now my nightly runs when he texted me. The moment I saw his name on the screen, I opened the message. I hadn't heard from him in too long, I was starting to think I wouldn't hear from him again. Though four days ago I was seemingly okay with it, I realized I'm not. I like the arrangement we have. Then, after ignoring my message for days, he sends me a text telling me he's bleeding. What was I supposed to do? I went straight to my sister's room and asked her where the Football House was. Then, despite being exhausted from all the running, I rushed downstairs, got in my car, and drove straight here.

I pick up the blue jersey he's referring to from the floor and add alcohol to it. "Sit down," I instruct.

He obeys, sitting on the edge of his bed. I walk up to him and stand between his legs. I bring the jersey up to his face slowly. When it touches his skin and he doesn't flinch, I take that as my chance to get started cleaning up the blood.

I sigh, suddenly hit by a wave of exhaustion. "You okay?" Nick asks.

"I'm tired and—" I start but stop.

"Tired and what?" He presses.

"Tired and wondering why in the world you'd get drunk and get into a stupid fight," I reply and I can hear the annoyance in my voice.

He cracks a smile and I press the piece of clothing harder onto his face, "Ouch!" he says and I laugh. "Ahh, I see. That was intentional," he adds.

"No one told you to smile! I was being serious," I tell him.

"Well, I was smiling at the fact that you were worried about me," he replies.

I clean the last bit of blood from his cheek and watch as he bites his lips. I look away, trying to not dive into something I should avoid right now. "You shouldn't be fighting," I tell him.

"I've actually been fighting less since..." he stops mid-sentence.

"Less since what?" I ask.

He looks at me and his hands come up to rest on my hips. "Since..." he starts then shakes his head, "... since my brother is no longer here to bail me out," he finishes. Something tells me that wasn't what he was going to say. Or maybe that's just wishful thinking.

"Ohh, okay. Well, all done," I tell him, stepping back and causing his arms to drop. "Where do I put this?" I ask with the jersey hanging from my finger.

He stands up. "I've got it," he says, taking it from my hands. "Thank you."

"There wasn't a lot of blood and the cut was small, so it should heal without leaving a scar. A black eye is probably coming though," I warn him.

His eyes widen. "What are you, a doctor? I thought you were prelaw!" He tells me, surprising me a little by remembering my major. I told him I wanted to be a lawyer when we first started talking. I guess I shouldn't be shocked that he actually listens to me.

"I am. But Elia is injury prone, so I've had to tend to too many injuries," I tell him.

He walks over to the closet where I assume his dirty clothes hamper is. "Well, I'm glad I was able to use those skills tonight. Big thanks to your little sister!" he says, walking back.

"I guess so. Even though I'm only older—"

"By five minutes," he finishes, surprising me yet again. "That's about the same time difference between Kaitlyn and me and she'll never let me live it down," he tells me, walking back toward where I'm still standing next to his bed.

"So," I start lingering. "I guess you're good and alive, which is what I wanted to know," I say, getting ready to leave.

"I'm alive," he repeats. "thanks to you!" he adds.

I look down at my fingers as I try to figure out how to phrase my question. "Are you still mad at me or are we over that?" I ask, wondering if he'll go back to ignoring me.

He gives me that blinding smile, which makes me forget all about the rules I have in place. "Do you know why I was mad at you?" he asks.

"Because I said we weren't going to have a game night?" I reply half-jokingly.

He steps closer to me and I step back until the back of my legs press against the bed, so there's nowhere else for me to go. "You treat me like a piece of meat," he replies, his words a mixture of honesty and hurt.

"We had an agreement," I whisper.

"No feelings. No relationships. No public anything, I know," he starts. "But then again, you came looking for me tonight."

I didn't miss the look in the guys' eyes tonight when I stepped into the house looking disheveled while searching for Nick Hunter, The Nick Hunter. I can't pretend I didn't hear them whistle as I made my way to the backyard and toward his room. "I'm not looking to be in a relationship," I tell him, trying to stay true to my original intentions.

"I know. I don't want a relationship either," he says. For some reason, him not wanting a relationship with me makes my stomach turn. This is all too confusing. I don't want him but am not happy to learn he wouldn't want me.

"Okay, so we agree," I say, "We're on the same page."

His fingers brush against my own as he takes my hand in his. "But I'm still a person. A pretty decent one if you ask me."

I smile, loving the way his hand feels on mine. I've missed that feeling. "Would the guy you fought say the same?" I ask, laughing.

He shrugs, "Maybe after a few drinks?"

"I doubt it!" I joke.

The smile leaves his face. "Be serious with me for a second. I know I'm rarely ever serious but I mean this." At his words, my stomach sinks. I'm not sure where he's going next.

"Well, you're drunk, so it makes sense that you'd do something totally out of character," I joke nervously.

"Amelia," he says, pinning me down with his eyes.

I take a deep breath, feeling electricity course through my body. "Sorry. I'll be serious, go ahead," I tell him, feeling like something important is about to happen. I find myself wanting to run from it and toward it at the same time.

He caresses my fingers and that relaxes me a little. "I don't want to feel like your dirty little secret. We don't have to tell people what's going on between us, even though your sister already knows. But we can be friends or at least pretend to be. I may not be the greatest guy, but I'm at least good at game night," he finishes.

I stand there taking his words in. What he's asking from me is not unreasonable. "We can try the friends thing," I tell him. Treating him like a friend is the least I can do.

He makes a big show out of taking a deep breath. "Thank goodness! You had me in suspense this entire time. I've never asked a girl to be friends with me before," he says, and I laugh, feeling the tension dissipate.

"Makes you wonder why you'd start to now," I say.

His right hand moves to my cheek. "I guess I must like you," he whispers and then his lips are on mine. I close my eyes and take it all in, even the taste of tequila that lingers. I try not to think too deeply into his words.

His hands start roaming over my body, distracting me, but before he has a chance to take my shirt off, I open my eyes and take a step back. "Well, I'll let you sleep," I tell him, not missing the lust in his eyes.

"Or you could sleep here," he says as he closes the distance again and tries to kiss me. I stop him before he has a chance.

I think of the perfect response. "Tonight, I was here as your friend and nothing more. So, yeah, I hope you wake up tomorrow without a crazy hangover or a black eye. Drink lots of water. Goodnight!" I tell him, then I'm rushing out the door and heading out the same way I came in, except this time, I have a huge smile on my face.

# 12

## AMELIA

I wake up with a pounding headache. It's almost as if I were the one who got so drunk last night that I ended up fighting someone. If I feel like this, I can't imagine how Nick must feel today since he's the one who actually did all that.

I came home last night after tending to football guy and found myself restless. Instead of shutting down so I could sleep, my mind was working on overdrive wondering what this new arrangement meant. Just sex, I could do, but now we're supposed to be friends and I have no clue what a friendship with Nick will be like. Is it even possible to just be friends with him?

A knock on my door startles me. "Leave me alone, Elia!" I shout, not ready to be awake just yet.

"Come out!" she shouts back. I sit up on my bed knowing if I don't get up and open the door, she'll linger just outside of it and continue to yell at me. "I don't know why you always lock your door, only you and I live here, you know!" she adds.

I've told her a million times why I lock my door. If there's a burglar, it's just an extra layer of protection. I encourage her to lock her own door too. Speaking of doors, she knocks on it again more aggressively this time. "Hurry up!"

"I'm coming," I shout back. I take my sweet time getting up from my bed. When I open the door, my sister's no longer standing on the other side of it. I walk past her room when I see it's open and then toward the living room to figure out what it is that my sister so desperately wanted from me. I could've still been lying on my bed thinking about—"Nick, what are you doing here?" I ask when I see him and my sister seated on the couch. They're literally sitting in the exact same place as they were on Tuesday. Before I ruined it all. Before everything changed again.

He turns to look at me, smiling deviously. I inspect him and am surprised to find no black eye. "Your face looks good," I tell him.

My sister's giggle makes me aware that my words taken out of context sound like a compliment. "Thank you," he says, accepting the compliment I didn't mean to give.

"No! Ugh, I mean... there's no black eye," I explain.

"Ahh! So that's why you asked where the football house was," my sister says.

I nod. "Nick got into a fight."

"Aw, did you piss him off enough to make him go pick a fight with someone else?" My sister's words surprise me. I don't know why I hadn't thought about that. There's no way he would've picked a fight because we argued. Would he?

I look at him, hoping he can answer my silent question.

"Your sister and I are good now," he tells her with grin. "So, I decided to come by and bother you guys."

I look at him, confused. It's too early for this. "You didn't even give us a heads up," I tell him.

"We're friends now. This is how I treat my friends," he replies.

"You guys are something else," my sister says, seemingly over our arrangement.

I shake my head. "You just show up at your friends' houses unannounced?"

"Yup!" he says. "So, what are we doing today, guys? I have to go to my dad's later today but my morning is free. Anyone up for breakfast? I make great eggs," he says, and I can't tell if he's joking. He seems really excited for a person I expected to wake up with a huge hangover.

"Sign me up!" my sister says.

He looks at me and I know he's searching for a reaction. He's waiting to see if I'll lash out or welcome him in. "I mean, if you're going to show up at my house in the morning unannounced, as my friend, the least you can do is make me breakfast," I joke, and I don't miss the relieved look on his face.


## NICK

MY MORNING GOES BETTER THAN I EXPECTED. HONESTLY, IF I DIDN'T have to go to Dad's for our family Sunday, I wouldn't be putting on my pants right now and getting ready to leave.

I'm not saying the morning was great because of how it ended, though that played a big part, but because I got to have breakfast with Amelia and her sister.

I look down at Amelia, who is on the bed asleep. I'm glad I woke up before my alarm went off, which was great since I didn't want to wake her up. She needs her rest.

Putting on my shirt, I can't help but smile. My mind goes back to a couple hours ago. To the look on her face when she saw me on her couch this morning. I wanted to thank her for checking in on me last night. For making sure I was okay. I also had to make up for not seeing her for almost a week. I needed to see her and take advantage of this new 'friendship agreement'. Of the opportunity to get her to see me as more than just someone she sleeps with. I want her to see me as a person. A person she could spend time with outside, and not just inside, the bedroom.

I made her and her sister eggs. Then, we started watching a movie. Before the movie ended, Elia left to hang out with some of the cheerleaders. Then it was just Amelia and me. We didn't rush off to the bedroom. Instead, we hung out in the living room like friends would. We finished the movie and talked about classes. I got to learn more about her, including why she wants to be a lawyer. Amelia wants to change the world.

I admire that. It makes me look up to her even more. She's got a good head on her shoulders and any man would be lucky to be with her. I'm lucky to get her to give me the time of day.

Eventually, Amelia and I decided to move over to her bedroom and well, that was that.

Putting on my shoes, I open her door slowly and quietly. "Heading out already?" I hear a sleepy Amelia say from behind me.

"I would love to stay," I tell her. "But I can't," I add. Man, I've never wanted to skip family Sunday more than I do now. Staying in bed with Amelia all day is a million times better, but I can't bail on my dad.

She fixes her pillow, getting herself more comfortable. "Okay. Have fun," she says, then closes her eyes.

Unable to help myself, I walk toward the bed and place a soft kiss on her lips. I see her smile with her eyes closed. Before my thoughts get the better of me, I turn around and walk out the door.

As I walk out of her apartment, I get the feeling I didn't get yesterday after the win on the field, and it catches me off guard, just like Amelia does.

# 13

## AMELIA

It's been three weeks since Nick and I decided to be friends. Three weeks since he got into a fight and I went looking for him, making sure he was okay.

"What do you think about this one?" My sister says, walking into the room with her third costume of the day. This one is of Wonder Woman.

"I like it, but I thought you guys would all match?" I ask.

She nods. "We are! We get to be superheroes this Halloween," my sister says. Halloween is a little over a week away and my sister's been trying to get me to help her with her costume.

"It looks fine," I tell her.

She gives me an incredulous look. "I'll just wait for Nick to come and I'll ask him. You've said the same thing about every costume I've tried on so far."

"I hope you return the ones you won't use," I tell her.

"Or maybe you could wear one?" she says, smiling at me.

Ha ha. Very funny. "I will not be going to any Halloween parties, thank you very much!"

"Fine!" she says, turning around and walking out of my room. "Maybe Nick can convince you," she shouts on the way out and I laugh. Since we agreed that we'd try to make a friendship work, he's been coming over more often.

Oddly enough, Elia, he, and I have all been spending a lot more time together.

Three weeks have changed a lot of things for all of us. Honestly, even the first time we slept together, that Sunday after he made us breakfast, felt differently. Something about moving forward made everything feel more real. More intense. I guess you could also chalk it up to not using a condom, which was a first for us.

As the thought enters my head, so does another one. This one, though, isn't making me smile. Nope, it wipes the smile right off my face as I jump out of bed and look for my phone. I unlock it quickly and head over to the calendar.

---

I TAKE DEEP BREATHS THE ENTIRE WALK TO THE CAR. UNLOCKING THE door, I get in and put my seatbelt on. Then, I just sit there for a moment too long. I don't want these thoughts in my head. I don't want it to be true.

My heartbeat races.

My breath shortens.

My fear grows.

I shake it off. I try to, anyway. It's more like I push down the thoughts, turn the key, and start the engine. Then, I drive to the pharmacy. I shouldn't have encouraged that to happen.

I step out of the car and every step after that feels like it's being taken by someone else, not me.

*You're smarter than this,* the rational part of my brain tells me. I am smarter than my actions reflect. This is the worst-case scenario.

I don't want to think about any of it. Not right now. Not when I need to continue. I just have to move forward. Entering the pharmacy, I look at the aisle tags and find the one I'm looking for. I walk toward it slowly, trying to breathe with every step.

*It doesn't have to be worst case scenario,* I tell myself. I could be worrying for nothing. We're always smart. Even extra safe. Except this time. But still, I should be fine. I'm on the pill. People do that all the time and it works. One layer is fine, right? It works for other people. It works 99.9% of the time.

Finding what I'm looking for, I make my way to the cash register. I opt for the self-checkout instead of the cashier because I don't want them to be someone I know. Someone from school. I don't want someone judging me or worse, pitying me.

---

I GET HOME LATER THAN EXPECTED DUE TO THE FACT THAT I HAD TO keep pulling over on the side of the road because my vision would get blurry and I no longer knew where I was. It was dangerous to drive when I felt so close to blacking out, so I took my time. The longer I waited, the more panicked I became though.

Getting out of the car, I can't help but run toward the house. I don't greet the doorman. Don't bother taking the elevator. When I enter into my apartment and my sister says something to me, I ignore her and run to the bathroom instead. Locking the door, I head straight to the sink feeling ready to puke.

*The only way to stop panic is with information.*

*No reason to fear unless there's a reason to fear.*

*I won't know what to be scared of unless I do this.*

My phone pings just as I finish giving myself a pep-talk. Looking down at where I've set it on the sink counter, I see the name of the last person I want to think about sprawled on the screen.

**Football Guy:** What are you doing tonight?

I flip the phone over so I no longer have to stare at the screen.

Letting my head rest on the mirror, I let out a growl. It's not pretty. It's not normal. It's just my frustration manifested because I knew better and yet here I am in an unexpected position. I hope I'm not the .01%.

Emptying the plastic bag's contents into the sink, I throw the bag in the trash. Returning to the counter, my fingers grip the sides as I look down at the five pregnancy tests I've purchased.

Just in case.

Just. In. Case.

Then, before I get ready to pee on a stick, I send a prayer up to whomever is listening. Please let it be negative.

# 14

NICK

I exit the locker room feeling like I'm on top of the world. The feeling is made greater when the moment I'm out the facility, students and cars are everywhere cheering and chanting. When they see me, they yell my name, and hell if I don't enjoy it.

I'm damn good.

Easy to tell if you see me play.

Today, I won us the game. I mean, Lincoln made a really good throw threading the ball between two defenders, but I got enough separation to haul it in for the game-winning touchdown.

So, yeah, the chants were well-deserved.

"Hold up!" I hear someone scream from behind me and I immediately notice the voice as that of my teammate, Wright.

"What's up?" I ask, when he finally catches up. A smile still on my face as the crowd continues chanting our team name.

He rests his hand on my shoulder. "This is amazing," he replies.

I nod. "It gets like this," I tell the rookie. "At first, it's a slow build, but once the season gets going, the intensity of the fans picks up." It's like they appreciate the level of play more. I get that. It only gets more serious as the season goes on.

"This is pretty awesome," he says, awestruck.

"It is," I smile then wave at a group of girls who begin to squeal.

"Are we partying tonight?" One of the girls with my jersey on shouts, interrupting my conversation with the rookie.

"Hell yeah!" I tell her, feeling like I'm on a high that I won't come down from for a while.

She bites her lip. "See you there!" she replies, and I can tell in her eyes that she's got plans for us tonight. I told Amelia I wasn't doing anything with anyone else and I'm not about to change that. It's not like she forced me to, but I'd rather sleep with her than any other girl. Since the choice was all the others or her, I choose her.

The moment she comes to mind, the high I was talking about keeping starts to go away. I'm reminded that Amelia has ignored every message I've sent her way since yesterday morning. After she ignored three of my calls today, I decided I needed to give her some space. While it's not unlike her to ice me out for a couple of days, I haven't actually done anything stupid this time. Still, I don't want to jump the gun and seem desperate.

I can't help but wonder what's going on. The more time passes without hearing from her, the more I can't shake the feeling that something isn't right. I was looking for Elia so I could see if I could get any information out of her, but she wasn't at the game today, which makes it worse. If everything's okay, why would she miss the game? That girl loves cheering.

I try to quiet my thoughts. I haven't heard from Amelia for a day, not weeks. She's been studying for her midterms, so that could be keeping her distracted. Still, I mean, she usually gives me a heads up, she did during finals last spring.

I hope she's not mad at me for something I've said or she's heard. I mean, it wouldn't be the first time where miscommunication threatens people's relationships. Not that we're in a relationship.

"Let's party!" Wright says, and I realize I've zoned out. We walk through the crowds and toward the parking lot with guards around us. It's funny that when the game ends we need security, but we walk around the school every day without them. When we reach the lot, the guards standing there watching over the cars wave at us.

"Good game," the taller guard, Edward, says.

"Thanks!" Wright replies.

"Great catch," the other guard, Jared, says. Jared's been watching Bragan games on his phone since I met him. He told me he would watch even before the team was any good. At least he gets better quality now that our games are televised.

I nod. "I'm glad I hauled it in," I tell him, toning down my cockiness. "I'll see you at the House," I tell Wright, who is now having a full-fledged conversation with the other guard.

"See you, then," he says, pausing briefly and then returning to his conversation, a step-by-step retelling of everything that just happened, like the guard wasn't watching it.

As I start to drive in the direction of the House, I look down at my phone sitting on the passenger side seat. The feeling that something is wrong nags at me and, instead of taking a left toward the House, I take the right toward Amelia's house. Maybe she's done with me, though I don't see why she would be, but if that's the case, she'll have to tell me in person because I'm not going to sit here and worry, wondering why I have this bad feeling.

I just want to check in and make sure she's okay.

That everything is okay.

That we're okay.

She did that for me.

I arrive at her apartment a few minutes later. Stepping out of the car, I'm glad I took the time to take a shower immediately after the game instead of waiting to shower at home.

At least I smell good.

I take the elevator up to her floor. When it opens, I step out and walk straight to her apartment door.

I'm getting ready to knock on the door when my hand pauses mid-air. *What are you doing, Hunter?* I ask myself. I've never been needy. Never wanted a girl so bad that I'd be willing to walk over to her apartment after not hearing from her.

Then again, I've never not heard from a girl. I used to hear back from them so often I'd have to block them. Every day I block random girls who get my number because I was once stupid enough to post it up for the world. I haven't changed it because I really like my number —but that's beside the point. The point is that coming here to Amelia's house looks desperate. It doesn't just look desperate, it is desperate.

I walk the short distance of the hall as I figure out what to do next. I can knock on the door and have her think I'm obsessed with her. Or I can walk away and just wait for her to message or text me back.

*It's only been a day.* I pull on the strands of my hair as I weigh my choices.

I'm not sure what this feeling is that I'm feeling right now, but I don't like it. I want it gone.

I'll just say it's a friend worrying about another friend.

A friend checking in to make sure the other one is still alive. I mean, Amelia not answering and Elia skipping practice is worrisome.

She did come to my house after I told her I got into a fight and stopped responding to her messages. I didn't think she was desperate then, I just thought she cared about me.

We're friends now, so showing up for a friend isn't desperate. It wasn't when she did it and it won't be when I do it.

Making up my mind, I get ready to knock on the door when it just opens up before me. Elia stands on the other side with her arms crossed in front of her and her head shaking like a disappointed mother.

I push down thoughts of my mother before they take hold. "Are you just going to stand there?" Elia says, and I welcome the conversation because it shuts off every other thought I shouldn't be having right now.

# 15

## NICK

"I just got here," I tell her. I don't know why I lie, but the thought that she was watching me as I argued with myself makes me feel like an idiot.

Elia looks at me knowingly. "I've been watching you walk back and forth in the hallway pulling your hair for a few minutes now." Well, there's no denying that.

"No, you haven't," I argue pointlessly. "I wasn't pulling my hair," I tell her.

She nods. "Yeah, you were. You probably didn't notice because you were too stressed about coming inside."

I shrug. "Should I be stressed out about coming inside?" I ask, wondering why she'd even be standing on the other side of the door watching me instead of letting me in. "Why weren't you at the game?" I ask.

"Have you talked to her?" she responds, the smile leaving her face. Elia is always smiling and the fact that she's standing on the other side of the door with a concerned look on her face makes me feel like something really is wrong.

I shake my head. "Is she okay?" I ask.

"You should come inside," she says, moving aside so I can enter through the door. I don't know what the hell is going on here, but it's definitely not making me feel like things are okay.

"Can you just tell me what's going on?" I ask, wanting to finally hear it.

"She's in her room, you can find her there," Elia says, then, in a surprising move, she walks out the front door and closes it behind her, leaving me standing in the living room.

I take the very known path over to Amelia's room. I knock on it tentatively when I arrive. "Are you in there?" I ask jokingly. "Come on, I know you're in there!" I say a few seconds later.

More time passes and I start to wonder if Elia pulled a prank on me. If she just made me stay in this house on my own to get back at me for something. Maybe Amelia isn't here.

Still, I can't shake the weird feeling I've had since last night. I really wish I had a beer right now. I sway back and forth on the balls of my feet. Then, feeling impatient, I knock again.

"Go away!" A voice I could never forget screams from the other side.

Why is she telling me to go away? Is this her way of stopping what we have going on? That's a very odd way to do it if you ask me. "Just open the door," I tell her. I test the handle to see if the door is unlocked; it's not.

"Leave!" she screams again. I've never heard this tone from her before. She's never really been angry when I'm around. She couldn't possibly be angry at me right now. I haven't done anything wrong. Then again, what people say I do versus what I actually do can vary and she may have gotten an earful of that.

"I swear to you nothing you've heard actually happened!" I tell her, trying to cover my bases. She should know I haven't done anything with anyone else... I told her that. "I told you the truth when I said I wasn't sleeping around anymore," I add.

"Please, just... just go away," she says, her voice cracking toward the end, and that's enough to suck all the humor out of the situation.

"Are you okay? What's going on?" I know for sure something is wrong. Amelia is the only girl I know who basically walks around wearing armor. She's tough as nails. Tough as they come. I wouldn't be surprised if she knocked any of the football players on any team on their ass. She's that strong. So the crack in her voice means something.

"Just leave," she says, and I can tell she's on the verge of tears.

I refuse to listen to her though because she's been there for me. She's cleaned up blood from my face. We're friends. The least I can do is be here for her when she seems to be going through something. God, if someone actually did something to her, I may be reacquainting myself with jail.

I knock on the door, more insistently this time. "I'm not going away, so just open it."

I wait for her to tell me to go screw myself. Instead, I hear a click of the door.

# 16

## NICK

I walk through the doors and take in her appearance. She looks lifeless. Like someone who just got out of the worst fight of their lives. There are shadows under her eyes and tears on her face.

The moment she looks at me she crosses her hands over her midsection. A protective stance. "What's going on?" I ask, stepping closer so she doesn't shut the door on my face and send me packing once again.

"You should go," she says, her words tentative.

I step farther in this time. Not giving her the slightest of chances to kick me out. I've learned that I shouldn't walk away from people when they look like they need me. My brother was always there for me. While I'm sure Amelia has Elia, I'm here for her too.

"I won't go. Something is clearly wrong. I'm not leaving you until I know you're okay," I tell her, trying to fight back the urge to ask her who hurt her—to ask who made her cry. So I can make them suffer.

She turns around and walks toward her bed. Sitting on the edge, she lifts her legs up and rests her head between her knees. "This is stupid."

"What is?" I ask, wondering if she thinks talking to me is a bad idea.

She sighs, lifts her head, and uses her hand to get rid of the tears streaming down her cheeks. I can tell something is weighing on her deeply. "I messed up," she starts.

"How?" I ask and then tell myself to stop asking questions. To just let her talk. I try to think about what my sister would tell me to do. She'd tell me that Amelia will tell me at her own pace. I should hang out with my sister more often.

I watch as her eyes water again. "I... I really... I shouldn't have... you..." her words don't make sense, but I definitely know I'm part of this because that's the last word she said. Me. Me, what? I have no idea what I did. I haven't seen her in days.

It unsettles me to see her crying. If you'd ask me a couple of days ago, I would've said she was incapable of doing such a thing. But right now, she looks like the world is collapsing before her and all I want is to hold her in my arms and tell her it's all going to be okay. Whatever it is. Except I'm afraid to touch her because I feel like I'm part of the problem—a problem I'm trying to figure out.

So instead, I do the dumbest thing I can do. I just stand there looming over her like a damn tree. Helpless to make her feel better until I know what she's actually going through.

"I want to help," I say when she doesn't say anything else. I take short steps toward her, hoping to close the distance between us. "But I need to know what's going on. I can't help you if I don't know."

Right as I'm about to reach her she shoots up from the bed, walks around me and out the door. I stay there frozen in place, wondering what to do next. Just as I'm about to follow behind her, she walks back in. She tosses something on the bed behind me.

"What's going on with you?" I ask.

She points at the bed and I turn back to look at what she's pointing at. "What is it?" I ask.

"Just read it," she says.

I get closer to the object. I don't miss the words on the label. They're right there for me to read.

*Pregnant.*

And despite how clear that word is, they leave me more confused than ever.

## AMELIA

I CAN TELL THE MOMENT HE READS THE WORDS SPLAYED ON THE STICK. I wish I had had the guts to tell him, but I don't. Because I can't get myself to say the words out loud. Because I can't stop myself from crying. It's the most pathetic thing I've ever seen, me like this.

But I can't help it because being pregnant was not part of the plan —my plan. At least, not this early in my life. Not like this. It was supposed to be law school, then dream job, and later on a husband and kids.

"What is this?" he asks. "Is this true?" he questions, his back to me as he inspects the stick. I asked myself the same question over and over again.

"I've taken five tests..." I tell him. Every time it said pregnant, I wished it didn't. I took every test hoping, praying, begging, and waiting for one of them to say that it wasn't true. All my begging was for nothing because nothing I could say was going to change the result. "I went to the hospital and they confirmed it," I add. The doctor said that it happens sometimes. That nothing is ever 100% effective.

"How could this..." he starts, unable to finish his question.

I take a deep breath, trying to hold back the tears. "Sex," I tell him.

"You said you were on the pill," he replies, finally turning away from my bed and facing me.

I nod. "I am."

"How could you be pregnant if you're on the pill?" he asks again, his voice regaining some of the strength it had lost after he saw the result. His face is pale and I can see the same scared look in his eyes that I've had in mine since yesterday. "How long have you known?" he asks.

"I found out yesterday," I tell him, finding the strength from within to speak.

"Yesterday?" he asks.

I nod.

"You've known since yesterday," he repeats, but it feels less of a question and more of a statement. "And you didn't tell me?" he finishes.

I sigh. "I had to process it first."

"And how's that going for you?" he asks, his words short.

"Clearly not well," I tell him, trying to maintain some form of composure.

His hands move to his hair as he starts to pull at his strands. Then he paces back and forth nervously. Anxiously. Angrily. "You said you were on the pill..." he repeats. I remember when it happened too, the Sunday he came to the house and made my sister and me breakfast. I've been on the pill every single day since the time I turned seventeen and my mother swore she wouldn't become a grandmother too soon. She learned from having us at a young age.

Oh no, my mom. How will she...? What will she...?

I can't let myself go there right now.

One battle at a time.

I feel anger start to rise from within me. "The pill isn't 100% effective," I tell him. "It's only 99.9%."

"And you had to be the lucky .01%?" he asks, and I don't miss the accusation in his voice. "Is it ours?" he asks. "Is it mine?" he clarifies.

I close my eyes and try to hold it together, but I'm afraid I'm about to lose it. Sometimes it's easier to be angry than sad. I speak through gritted teeth as I try to hold back the anger that's coursing through me. "You were the only one I was sleeping with."

"You said that, but how do I know for sure? God, everyone warned me about getting a jersey chaser pregnant. It's the lottery ticket move.

I should've known better," he says all this to himself as he paces back and forth, not knowing the effect his words are having on me. Not realizing how harsh they are.

Did he really just call me a jersey chaser? Did he accuse me of getting pregnant on purpose to get him to what, support me for the rest of my life? Is he serious?

I laugh but it's humorless. "No, actually, I should've known better. Get the hell out!" I yell.

"What?" he says, seemingly surprised at my reaction. "We have to figure this out!"

"You just accused me of intentionally getting pregnant so I can get you to what? Share your future millions of dollars with me? Golden ticket, that's what you think I want. You'd think I'd want to be pregnant for that?" I start walking toward the living room, knowing he'll follow behind. "I've never wanted nor needed anyone else to support me. The only reason I even gave you a second look was that I knew I could never have something serious with you. And you think I'd want to have your child? On purpose? I've worked my ass off here. Without tutors. Without rich daddies. Without the school worshipping the ground I walk on. I've worked hard to prepare myself to go to law school and all my plans could go to shit because of this and you dare sit here and accuse me of wanting this?" The words rush out of my mouth.

I stop when I reach the front door and turn around. "That's not what I meant," he says, looking embarrassed, ashamed, perhaps remorseful. Too little too late.

Opening the door, I make sure there's no weakness in my voice when I speak. "Get. Out. Now," I tell him.

He gets ready to open his mouth again, but I shake my head. He looks back toward the room then at me. Finally, he does as he's told and walks out the door.

The moment he does, I slam it shut and collapse on the floor.

# 17

## NICK

I leave Amelia's house and drive around until the guys tell me the party's started. A party. That's what I need right now. Alcohol and chaos on the outside to stop the inside wheels from churning. To stop my thoughts from driving me insane.

Pregnant.

How could she be? I mean, I know how pregnancy works, but I'm supposed to be better than this. *You could've been smarter.* My mother's voice plays in the back of my head. Not sure why she's the first person to come to mind right now, but I don't like it one bit. She shouldn't be teaching anyone lessons; she's done way worse.

But Amelia. She's smarter than I am. Even if I failed, she wouldn't have. Unless she wanted to? That's a dumb ass thought, but I can't stop myself from thinking it.

Alcohol.

Yup.

That and music is what I need right now. I need to blackout and get the fact that I'm going to be a father out of my head.

Can you imagine what my brother will think? My sister? The guys on the football team? Dad. I mean, I guess they wouldn't be super surprised since I am me after all. But still. I can't be a father. I've seen my dad worry and suffer. I'm not cut out for that. I mean, maybe in the future but certainly not now. Not at twenty-one years old.

I GET TO THE HOUSE A FEW MINUTES LATER AND AM MORE EXCITED THAN I should be about being greeted by a bunch of strangers. They pat me on the shoulder. They try to talk to me about the game and whatever else, but I'm not paying too much attention.

Cutting the people trying to talk to me short, I head straight toward the kitchen where cold beers and liquor await. I don't even know what to drink first.

Looking around at all the drinks that have been compiled, I pick the strongest thing I can find and just down it straight from the bottle. When I start feeling buzzed, I allow myself to take in my surroundings again. The house is full, just as it usually is for a victory party. I'm not feeling like a winner right now.

I take another gulp then bring the entire bottle with me to the living room.

I find the guys and pretend to listen to the jokes and stories they tell. I try to enjoy the moment, the lightness that comes from being buzzed because, I know that when I wake up tomorrow, a hangover won't be the worst thing I'll be facing.

---

"YOU NEED TO STOP!" I HEAR SOMEONE YELL. I STOP TO LOOK AT WHO says that and that's when a punch lands on my mouth. Instantly, I taste the blood. I look down and see one of the hockey guys beneath me and remember that's what I've been doing—fighting. Why do I always do this? Why is it always a hockey player? Why do they keep coming back? Man, I have a lot of questions.

I dodge a punch then throw one of my own. I'm not sure how this fight started, honestly don't remember much of today already. All I know is picking fights with hockey guys seems to be Drunk Nick's favorite thing to do. Sober Nick wakes up hurting from it. Not that I'm not strong or tough, because I am, but hockey players aren't a walk in the park either. They give me a run for my money, even though I catch them at the end.

He flips over so I'm caught under him. His hand raises and just as he's about to hit me straight in the face again, someone pulls me him away while someone else pulls me up.

I turn back and am greeted by a familiar face. "Lincoln?" I say out loud. Shocked that the rookie would show up to the party. He rarely parties with us.

Before he has a chance to answer, the hockey guy stands up and charges at Aron, I guess angry that he got in the way of our fight. I take a page from our defense and tackle the guy back down to the ground. No one hurts the quarterback, that's the rule.

I hear the sounds of people screaming, but I'm wrestling back and forth for the upper hand in this fight, so I can't focus on what they're saying. Multitasking is hard when you're this drunk. I finished more than one bottle tonight, that's for sure.

I glance around the room briefly when the sounds get louder and louder. I realize others are fighting too. I guess I started a brawl. Thank goodness there's no furniture here to get damaged. Honestly, I'm not even sure why we care about the furniture so much. It's not like it's expensive.

It could be the alcohol or a black eye starting to form, but my vision suddenly becomes blurry. I'm pulled from the floor again and dragged somewhere by someone. I try to wiggle out of their hold but a second person joins them in holding me and I can't break loose. The wind hits me out of nowhere and that's when I realize we're outside.

Then, I see lights.

Red. Blue. Flashing.

Just as I realize what's happening, I'm thrown into the back seat of a police cruiser. Not going to lie, the first thought in my mind is that Colton isn't here to bail me out. Who am I supposed to call now?

# 18

## NICK

I t takes about two hours, I think, for me to start feeling like I'm more tipsy than drunk. I sit in the cell with my head resting against the wall wondering what to do next. Who to call? I know any of the guys would come and get me if I asked them to but I hate the idea of asking. I'm surprised I'm the only one here right now. You'd think with the brawl I thought was happening that a bunch of us would get arrested. Maybe I imagined it?

I hear the chatter of two officers from the hall. I get up and walk closer. "Excuse me!" I say, and the way the words leave my mouth tell me there's still a heck of a lot of alcohol left in my body.

One of the officers walks over and sighs loudly when he reaches me. Oh, I recognize him! "Hi, Officer Smith," I greet him with a big smile, hoping that earns me brownie points and he lets me out of here.

The other officer leaves the room and then it's just Smith and me.

I guess it was a slow night for crime. "Don't give me that crap!" he says, and I instantly frown. Why does he sound so upset?

"It was just a stupid fight," I tell him. "I have no idea how it started. I'm pretty sure it wasn't my fault," I add, hoping that makes it better somehow.

He shakes his head like my father would. I mean, I recognize the dude but not enough for him to look this pressed about my current situation. "That's the problem with you," he says.

"It wasn't that big a deal," I tell him.

"Tell that to the kid's face," he adds and I hold back a smile. I can't say I'm not somewhat proud that I did some damage. "And yours," he adds, and almost as if I couldn't feel anything till that moment, my face starts to hurt.

He steps away and I feel like I'm losing him. I gotta convince him to let me out. He has before. Usually, he just lets my brother pick me up without me being charged. I need that again. Especially now. My current strategy isn't working, so let me try something different. "I'm sorry," I reply, half-meaning it.

He stops in his tracks. "You kids have a whole future ahead of yourselves and here you are wasting it," he says, sounding like someone who has some regrets.

"I don't know what got into me today," I tell him, then every part of me remembers the one thing I wanted to forget. "Actually, I do know..." I start and then wonder if I should mention this at all. Is a random police officer really the first person I want to tell? "I may become a dad," I tell him, feeling like I have to tell someone.

"Okay," he says and I realize that wasn't the clearest way of saying it.

I try again. "A girl I've been seeing told me today that she's pregnant," I clarify.

"Is it yours?" he asks, and part of me feels some satisfaction at realizing someone else had the same question I did.

I shrug. "She says it is."

"Do you have any reason to doubt her?" he asks, and the way he asks his question makes me think about it in a different light. Did I believe her when she said it? Not entirely. Do I have a reason to doubt her? Not at all.

I shake my head. "It caught me off guard though," I tell him, finding this conversation really soothing for some odd reason.

"I get that," he says. "Do you love her?"

I start coughing. "I'm sorry, what?" What kind of a question is that?

"Do you love her?" Officer Smith asks again. I heard his question the first time around. I just, I've never been asked that before.

The officer who left earlier returns. He's good to go," the officer says, pointing at me.

I look back and forth between the two of them. "But I didn't call anyone," I tell them. Not sure why I'm arguing against leaving. This just wasn't the way I thought it would happen.

"The QB is here for you," he says then turns around and walks out the way he walked in.

My brother's here? How the heck did he know? Officer Smith opens the cell door and escorts me out.

When we reach the lobby, I find that the quarterback waiting for me isn't Colton, it's Lincoln. That shouldn't be shocking, but I was really hoping it was my brother—however ludicrous that thought was. I guess this one isn't so bad.

"You came to get me out?" I say, a little bit shocked.

He nods. "We're teammates," he says. "I couldn't leave you here forever, now could I?"

"Not if you want to win," I say, giving him the douchey-est of smiles.

He shakes his head but I can tell he was about to crack a smile. "Let's go," he says, turning around and walking toward the exit. I follow behind him.

Aron Lincoln may not be Colton but right now he definitely reminds me of him. Who thought the walk-on freshman I hated at the beginning would be the one bailing me out tonight? Certainly not me. But I guess today is just full of surprises.

## 19

NICK

I find myself sitting in my living room next to my sister a week later. "I knew it! I knew it would be you. It had to be. I'm just surprised it didn't happen sooner," she exclaims. It's family Sunday, and despite the raging hangover from yet another victory party, I still had to be here. I skipped last week because of the bruises on my face. I told Dad I had gotten a beating the night before in the game and was going to take Sunday to rest instead. I wasn't about to explain waking up in jail and with a black eye.

"Keep it down, will you? Dad's going to hear," I tell her. We're at home getting ready to make our usual family dinner a family lunch instead. Colton's playing in New England tonight and we're watching the game live. So, instead of canceling, family day gets made longer, which sucks because I'm still trying to wrap my head around the fact that Amelia is pregnant. It's been a week since she told me. A week since I've heard from her.

Kaitlyn looks toward the dining room where Dad is setting up the table. Then she turns to me and whispers. "So, which jersey chaser is it?" she asks, and I can tell she's enjoying herself a little too much, while I'm getting ready to pass out.

"She's not a jersey chaser," I correct. "Don't call her that." I instantly realize how much of a hypocrite I am. A week ago, I called Amelia that myself. In my defense, I was shocked, surprised, stunned even. Still, that's no excuse for basically telling her I thought she did it intentionally. That's not at all what should've come out of my mouth. Shouldn't have been in my head. But my mouth spoke before I could process. I don't even know how to talk to her again.

I've picked up my phone a million times since last week and have set it back down each time. She's going through the hardest time in her life and I made it worse. I don't think they make cards for that. It'd be a lot easier to give her a *Sorry I'm an asshole* card instead of apologizing personally. I'm sure Amelia would set it on fire before she read it.

"Hello, are you there?!" Kaitlyn says, annoyingly snapping her fingers in front of my face.

I push her hands away. "What?" I ask, knowing I missed whatever million things she just said.

"What are you going to do now?" she asks.

"The hell if I know!" I say louder than I should.

Kaitlyn's expression becomes serious. "You should tell Dad."

"Tell Dad what?" the person who shouldn't be hearing this conversation asks as he comes into the living room. "Lunch is ready. Thanks for helping me set the table, by the way," he says sarcastically.

"We know how much you love to do it," Kaitlyn says, jokingly.

We get up from the couch and follow my father's lead. The moment we take our seats, Dad starts to speak. "So, what do you have to tell me?" Dad asks.

"Yeah, Nick. What do you have to tell Dad?" Kaitlyn echoes. I have no clue why I told her in the first place. I guess I needed someone to talk to, someone other than a random cop. Still, next time something blows up my life, my sister will be the last to hear about it. She's enjoying herself too much. I think she thinks this gets her a pass to do whatever she wants since she'll never be a bigger disappointment than I am.

I think about whether I want to tell Dad right now. "What's going on? Are you going to tell me I'm going to be a grandpa or something?" My dad jokes, and if I had started eating or drinking, I'd be choking right now.

Kaitlyn starts laughing so hard I kick her from under the table. "Ouch!" she complains.

My dad looks from her to me. "Is that it?" he says.

I wish he didn't become the kind of father who pays attention. Right now, the one who barely knew what was going on in our lives would be preferable. I don't want to lie to him, but I'm also not ready to tell him the truth. Not right now. Not when I've screwed it all up. "I'm so hungry!" I say in a poor attempt to change the topic.

"Nick Hunter, did you get a girl pregnant?" My father asks, not letting it go. I guess I wouldn't let it go either if I were a father. Which I guess I will be. Damn.

I nod.

"When?"

"When did I get her pregnant? Isn't that too much information?" I say, trying to lighten the mood, but the delivery of the joke is dry because this isn't a joking matter.

My dad shakes his head. "When did you find out she was pregnant?" he says.

"Saturday," I tell him.

"Yesterday?" he asks.

I shake my head. "Last week."

"Who is she to you?" he asks.

I turn to look at Kaitlyn, who's playing with the food on her plate as she pretends to not be hanging on to every word spoken.

"She's just a girl," I tell him, the lie rolling off my lips.

"Just a girl? A random hook-up?" my dad asks, his correct use of the word *hook-up* throwing me off.

I shake my head, allowing myself to be honest. "We've been seeing each other for a while," I confess.

"How long?" he asks, and I feel like I'm in the middle of an interrogation.

"Eight months," I tell him, then hear Kaitlyn start to choke.

She probably should've held off on drinking her water. "Eight months!" she says in disbelief. I guess, knowing me, I wouldn't have believed it either.

"So, she's your girlfriend?" my dad says.

I shake my head again. "Not really."

"Are you sleeping with other girls as well?" my dad asks, and I hate that this is the conversation we're having right now.

"No," I say, my voice low.

Kaitlyn whistles. "She must be some kind of woman for you to drop the little chasers for her," Kaitlyn says and she's right. Amelia isn't like any of my other hookups.

"How is she taking this?" Dad asks. I'm surprised he's not angrier.

I close my eyes and take a deep breath. "She was freaking out. Then I screwed up, so right now she must be seething. And she probably never wants to see me again."

My dad pins me with a questioning look. "Do I want to know?"

I shake my head, knowing he'd be more disappointed in me right now if he knew.

"You going to fix it?" He asks, but I know it's less of a question and more of an expectation. I'm a Hunter. There's a lot that comes with that name.

I nod.

I turn to Kaitlyn, surprised she hasn't said anything. "Good. I know it seems impossible right now, but you can do this. I was your age when Colton came around," he says, reminding me and making me feel like less of a failure.

"Right, right! I almost forgot," I tell him, breathing a little easier now. "How did you react?" I ask, hoping he freaked out and called Mom all sorts of things too.

"I bought her a ring. We got married before Colton was born," he responds.

Married? I hope he doesn't think that's the way I'm going to fix this. I never imagined myself being married. Didn't imagine being a father either. "Look at how well that ended up." With my mom betraying my dad and extorting my brother.

My dad sets down his fork and places his hands, palms up, on the dining table. Kaitlyn and I take that as a signal to put our hands in his. Dad loves to do this. I used to fight against it but it's easier to just let it be. "I ended up with your brother and two of you. I couldn't be happier. I wouldn't trade that for anything."

I guess he's right. "You got double the trouble!" Kaitlyn shouts, finally breaking her vow of silence.

My dad chuckles. "Double the joy."

It's crazy how, despite how much my mom hurt my dad, he still looks at his time with her fondly because it gave him us. Inspiring to see that Dad wouldn't spare himself the suffering if it meant Kaitlyn and I wouldn't be here. That's love.

He got double the trouble. Considering Amelia is also a twin, I wonder if we'll double what we bargained for too.

## 20

NICK

With a lump in my throat and a few shots of tequila running through my body, courtesy of my sister, we arrive at Gillette Stadium. I head toward our assigned seats while Kaitlyn and Dad go and grab some snacks.

"What's up!? I didn't know you were coming!" I greet Chase when I see him sitting at the seat next to mine. I know he played on Thursday this week because whenever I'm not at practice, playing football, or with Amelia, I sit at home and watch all the guys play. I know their game schedules.

"Figured, since I was off, I could catch the game. See Colton and Zack in action, you know," he says, surprising me with how many words he strung together. Maybe the NFL has changed him.

I give him a man-hug. "You're getting big," I say, squishing his arms to apparently prove my point. I haven't seen him in person since graduation.

"Yeah, some summer weight and lots of workouts," he says, shrugging.

He looks behind me and I turn to find Dad and Kaitlyn with hotdogs and sodas trying to figure out where to go next.

"Chase? Is that you?" My dad says, finally reaching us.

"Yes sir, how are you doing?" Chase extends his hand to shake my father's but Dad pulls him in for a hug instead.

At that very moment, my sister drops her Coke and I burst out laughing. "Get it together, sis," I shout.

"Shut up, Nick!" She retorts. Oh, my sister. She thinks she's slick but I know. I know more than she thinks. I was there that day... way back in high school. The first time she dropped her soda in front of Chase.

I turn to watch Chase. He doesn't know that I know either. It's kind of funny if you think about it. He moves past my dad and toward Kaitlyn. Crouching down in front of her, he picks up the empty cup then passes it to her. "Hey," he says, his voice all low and whatnot.

Like watching a tennis match, I turn my attention to Kaitlyn, who blushes in return. Too easy. She takes the cup from his hand. "Hi, I'm going to go grab another," she says, turning around.

"I'll come with. I forgot to get some snacks for myself," Chase replies, following behind her.

Dad and I take our seats, making sure we leave the two on the edge for Chase and Kaitlyn. "This way we don't have to get up when they come," I tell Dad.

He smiles at me. "Don't worry, I know too," he says with a wink. Then we both start laughing. It's nice to let something else distract me. This game between the Patriots and Giants, between Zack and Colton, and adding Chase and Kaitlyn's never ending love drama, will be enough to keep my mind from thinking about the things I can't avoid for too long.

Amelia.

Amelia and the pregnancy.

Amelia and my child.

Our child.

# 21

AMELIA

I press ignore on the incoming phone call for the tenth time today. I guess he isn't getting the clue, but he's known for brawn not brains. Yes, that was mean but not as mean as the words he said to me almost two weeks ago.

"You can't ignore him forever," my sister says, taking the seat next to me on the couch. She hands me a cup of tea and I relish the warm feeling of it in my hands. Ever since finding out I was pregnant, I've felt cold. Chills running through my body like I somehow transported myself to the Arctic and have nothing to cover me from the winds.

I guess that's the anxiety.

The fear.

The disappointment.

Anger.

At myself mostly. And a little angry at him too. Well, maybe a lot angry. "I definitely can," I tell her.

She fixes the covers over me. She's been taking care of me lately. She gets home from class and practice and just sits with me. "No, you can't," she says.

I hate that she's right. I have to talk to him about it at some point, even if it means not talking to him ever again after that. "I can for right now." I'm not ready to face his judgment again.

"So, what are you going to do?" my sister asks the dreaded question. The question I've asked myself over and over again.

I set the mug of tea on the table. "I don't know," I tell her the answer I've landed on over the last few days. I can't believe it's already been over a week. Ten days to be exact since my world was turned on its side and everything fell apart.

Elia sits on the couch then pats her lap with her hand and I take that as my clue to lie on her. All our differences aside, my sister is the one person I can always count on. "Isn't this nuts?" I say, looking up at her.

She runs her fingers through my hair. "Definitely unexpected if you ask me. I thought I'd be knocked up before you," Elia replies and I laugh. I can't help it. I thought the same thing.

"Honestly. You and me both. I would've put money on it." My plan was to go to law school. Then meet someone, perhaps a lawyer. Then maybe children. This jumps way too many steps on my plan.

My sister sighs loudly. "Are you going to tell Mom?" I feel the weight of the question the moment it leaves her mouth.

Suddenly, my mouth is dry and I feel like I'm struggling to breathe. I have pushed down thoughts of telling Mom since I realized I'd have to break the news to her. "Oh God, oh God," I say, getting up from the couch like it's on fire. I start pacing around the living room. "How am I going to tell Mom?" I question in all out panic.

"She isn't going to be mad at you," my sister says, but she and I both know that's not true. She's going to be livid. Disappointed too. She got knocked up by an athlete in college, our biological dad. He wasn't there for her. She raised us on her own until she met Steve. She wanted different for us.

"No athletes. That's the rule," I remind her of our mom's instructions. Funny that I usually tell my sister that as a joke. I didn't think it would ever apply to me. "Nick is a football player," I say out loud. "I got knocked up by an athlete despite Mom's warnings!" I shout again. How will I deal with Mom's disappointment for repeating the same mistakes she did even after she cautioned us against it?

"Calm down," my sister says as she gets up and walks toward me. When she reaches me, she places both of her hands on my shoulders. "It'll be okay. Everything will be okay." Before I even have a chance to argue with her, we hear a knock at the door.

"I'll get it," she says, walking past me. The knot in my stomach feels so large that it may tear me apart. "Oh," Elia says when she looks to see who's at the other side of the door. Her reaction tells me everything I need to know.

"No," I tell her with a firm shake of my head.

"But you guys need to talk about this," she presses.

I shake my head profusely this time. "I tried talking to him about it," I tell her, sparing her once again from every hurtful word he said to me. Every unexpected remark. The way he questioned my character and intentions. I gave her a brief summary after she came back home and asked how it went but nothing more. For some reason, I didn't want to believe it myself, let alone repeat the words out loud.

"You guys have to figure out what you're going to do next," she says, and Nick knocks on the door once again.

I sit on the couch and cradle one of the throw pillows. "I'll figure it out on my own."

"You don't have to," she says. "You shouldn't have to," she adds. "This took two people."

"The decision will take just one," I reply.

"But is that what you want?" she asks knowingly.

"I don't know what I want," I tell her, resigned. I lie back. Elia takes that as a sign to open the door. I close my eyes, not bothering to even look at him.

"Thanks," I hear him say.

"Don't thank me. I want to rip your eyeballs from your face," Elia says, surprising me with her anger. She's supposed to be the nice one.

"I deserve that," Nick says, his voice less authoritative than usual. Lower than usual too.

"You absolutely do," my sister replies. I hear the door close and feet padding closer. A few seconds later, I feel her hands on my shoulder. "I'll be in my room if you need me."

"Thanks," I tell her, sitting upright and finally opening my eyes. It's not like I can avoid this despite how much I want to.

I hear his footsteps and then watch as Nick comes to stand in front of me. "Should we go talk in your room?" he asks. I take in his appearance. He's wearing sweatpants and a hoodie, probably the first time I've seen him like this. I'm surprised to see shadows under his eyes. I guess this reality is weighing heavily on him too. *Or maybe he was just out partying again*, the more logical part of my brain says. Elia says the team did win on Saturday and every home victory is followed by a party. Nick's told me that himself.

"Being in my room didn't go so well the last time," I tell him, unable to stop myself from being petty. From reminding him of that day. I knew the news would be a shock to him but his reaction was totally uncalled for. He attacked my credibility, my character.

He hangs his head. "I know. I'm sorry."

I shrug. "Well, that makes it all better, doesn't it?" I reply sarcastically.

He sighs then sits next to me. I move over a little because I don't want to be that close to him. "I know it doesn't make it all better," he starts. "I shouldn't have said the things I said."

"Why? Because now I'm upset? Because I've ignored you?" I ask.

"Because they aren't true," he says, his words diffusing a little bit of my anger. I hold on to the rest because I'd rather feel anger than any of the other emotions wanting to take me over right now.


NICK


"Because you are none of the things I called you. It was all just so... unexpected," I tell her honestly.

"Welcome to the club," she replies sarcastically again.

I know I wasn't the only one to be caught by surprise. "You at least had a day to process it. I came to your house to see if you were okay, because I hadn't heard from you and your sister wasn't at the game, only to find out you were pregnant with my child," I argue, frustration getting the best of me.

"Oh, so now it's your child?" she says in disbelief. I know she questions my newfound certainty.

Am I sure the child is mine? That was one of the questions that instantly came to mind when I found out. The question I asked myself the moment I walked out of here over a week ago. The same question that played on repeat as I took shot after shot at the Football House. Even every punch I landed on the hockey guy, or he landed on me, was followed up by the same inquiry. I couldn't get it out of my head. Jail didn't make it any better either. Is it my child? The answer, I'm certain of. And I think I have been since she told me, but I couldn't get myself to accept it just yet because then it was real.

"Absolutely," I tell her. The text conversations we had about sleeping with other people play on repeat in my mind. "I know it's my child."

"What changed your mind?" she asks.

"My mind didn't change, it just cleared" I tell her. "When you told me, I was shocked. I'm sorry I questioned you. I'm sorry I made you feel worse. I was just surprised. But I know you. I know you wouldn't lie to me. I know that you wanted this less than perhaps even I did." She has plans too. It's not just me.

She nods and I feel like I'm breaking through the wall I created. "You can say that again. I would've never planned this... to have kids... now. With you," she finishes. For some reason, the last part of her statement hurts more than my face did after my last fight. Not that I've thought about settling down and having a family, but I wouldn't mind starting a family with her in the future. I guess we have no choice now.

"Not much we can do about it now," I tell her. Even if neither one of us planned this, we're having a child. She's pregnant. We can't turn back now.

I watch as her hands rest on her stomach. When she sees me looking there, she pulls them away. "I have choices," she says.

I'm trying to decipher what she means, but in cases like this, I may as well just be straight up and ask. "What are the choices?"

"The same choices anyone else in my position would have," she says, and I wait for her to tell me what those are.

"I could give it up for adoption," she says.

I shake my head. "I wouldn't want any child of mine to be given up for adoption. I don't think I could live with that."

"I could have an abortion," she says, ignoring me, and those words shock me more than the initial ones did.

"You'd want to do that?" I ask, a headache forming in the back of my head.

She shrugs. "It would make it all go away."

"And things would go back to normal?" I ask but I don't believe that.

She shakes her head. "Things would definitely go back to normal for you," she says, and I notice how she didn't say how things would impact her. From what I've heard about abortion, which isn't a lot, some women are affected by it in an impactful way and others aren't. I don't know where she'd fall.

"Or we could keep it?" I say tentatively. I know it's her body and her choice. But I can't help at least give her my opinion. Tell her what I think and hope she takes that into consideration.

She sighs. "I never thought I'd be a single mom at twenty-one," she says, then laughs, but there's no humor behind it.

"I'm here," I tell her. "You're not alone."

"You're here now," she corrects. I have been gone for the last week, so there's that.

I can't fault her for thinking I'll leave again. I left before. "I'm here to stay. We can do this together," I try to convince her. I want her to believe me because I'm serious.

"You say that now. But soon enough, it won't be a hypothetical. It'll be a child," she argues.

I pull at the hairs on the back of my head. "We can figure it out. We're not the first people to be in this position and certainty won't be the last. People can make it work," I argue.

She shakes her head. "You have your plans for the future and I have mine."

"Who says we can't have it all?" I ask.

# 22

## AMELIA

"Who says we can't have it all?" he asks, and for some reason I feel like I can't be seated for this conversation, so instead I get up and begin pacing. I don't care that my sister can hear every bit of this conversation from the other side of her door.

"Please tell me how it would work? Huh? I'd go to law school somewhere and you'd be playing in an NFL team somewhere else while we're sharing custody of a child and trying to co-parent. Explain to me how that would work?" I ask, trying to show him it's not all rainbows and butterflies. It's a child. A human life. This decision isn't one we can take lightly.

In a matter of seconds, he's right in front of me. We stare at each other without saying anything. I see the hope in his eyes and for a second I wish I shared it. I wish I thought something like this would work.

"We can figure it out," he says, not answering any of my questions.

I shake my head. "It's not that easy. I don't want to be a single parent." I don't want the responsibility of raising a child, not right now.

"Marry me, then!" he shouts. I think his words shock me just as much as they shock him. The way he freezes in place with wide open eyes shows me he didn't mean to say that.

"You're crazy," I tell him, stepping back, not giving his statement any weight.

He shakes his head then takes tentative steps toward me. He gets so close it feels like we're only a breath away. "Maybe it's crazy. Maybe I'm a little crazy. And honestly, I didn't plan on saying that at all," he says.

"Oh, I know," I tell him, feeling a little bit of the tension ease. The problem is still there, but Nick's random proposal does a little to dissipate the chaos; it's comical in a way.

"But maybe it's not so crazy after all," he says, seemingly processing his own words.

"I'm sorry, what?" I ask.

"You don't want to be a single mom. I don't want our child to be put up for adoption. I also wouldn't want you to get an..." he starts but can't get himself to say the word.

I say it for him. "Abortion."

"Yeah. That. I mean, at the end of the day it's your choice and I'll respect it. But why don't we try this out," he brings his hand to my chin and tips my face upward.

I step back and his hand falls. "This isn't like buying a car or clothes. You can't just take it back if you don't like it. It's a child we're talking about here," I argue, trying to bring some sense into him.

"Let's do this, Amelia. Let's get married and have a baby," he says, and I wonder if he has a concussion because the words coming out of his mouth are nonsensical.

I roll my eyes and walk toward the other side of the room. "It's not that simple."

He reaches me again and I feel like we're in some type of dance for control. "But maybe it can be?" he says, and the certainty behind his words make me wish I could believe them too.

"Do you understand what you're saying?" I press. I move toward him this time instead of away.

His hands find mine. "We've been seeing each other exclusively for months."

"We didn't start this with the intent of getting married," I tell him.

He nods. "And you never thought about marrying someone like me," he says, and I can hear the disappointment in his voice. Why is he disappointed? Isn't that what we both agreed on?

"I'm sure getting married wasn't part of your plans either," I tell him.

It's his turn to agree. "I hadn't, but I wouldn't mind it with you." I think he meant his words to be some sort of compliment, but that's not how they feel.

He wouldn't mind? Marriage isn't something you settle for. This isn't something you just do. "That wouldn't even begin to address all the issues I said earlier. It's not even a choice."

"So, are you turning down my proposal?" he asks with a goofy smile on his face. I want to smack some sense into him and smile at the same time.

I wish I could be relaxed but the weight of the choices I have to make stop me. "I need time to think about what to do," I tell him, walking away from him and toward the couch.

I take a seat and Nick follows suit, sitting next to me. "Is keeping the child at least an option?" he asks, his legs bumping into mine. He still doesn't understand the magnitude of this.

"I'll think about it," I tell him. I have to think about everything. Every possible option.

He rests his hand on my knee. "Alright. Well, let me know if you need anything. If I can help you in any way. Like I said, if you want to do this—to raise this child together—I'll be right there with you."

"Thanks," I tell him as I think about the puzzle I have to figure out how to solve. His hand leaves my knee and starts making its way up until it rests on my belly.

"I'm here," he says, looking down. It feels awkward to have his hand there because it's an acknowledgement of what's happening. He removes his hand and his eyes find mine. "I'll give you time," he says, then gets up and walks out the door. As soon as the door closes behind him, I hear another one open.

# 23

AMELIA

"So, what did he say?" my sister asks.

"Have you just been in your room waiting for him to leave?" I ask, amused.

She nods. "Yeah. I mean... you're lucky I didn't put my ear to the door to listen. I actually had my headphones on to give you some privacy," she tells me, surprising me. I definitely expected her to be seated in the room listening to everything we were saying.

"Color me surprised," I tell her.

"You can't talk about surprises," she says, laughing. I'm not sure I'm at the point where I can laugh about this yet. "So, what did he say?" she asks.

"He wants me to keep the baby."

"Really?" she asks, surprised.

I nod. I get up from the couch and start walking toward my room.

"And what do you think?" she asks, following behind me.

"I don't really know what to do," I tell her. "He thinks we can raise it together."

"You and him?" she repeats, shocked.

I laugh because my sister's reaction is similar to what mine was. "Yup. According to him, we can do it together," I tell her, waiting for her to tell me he's wrong as I sit on my bed.

"Nick Hunter said that?" she says, dropping onto the beanbag in the corner of the room.

"Yup," I reply.

"The Nick Hunter?"

"Yes," I say again.

"The football player? The party animal? The fighter? The guy who doesn't take anything or anyone serious?" my sister finishes, and I'd be lying if I didn't say the last part stung a bit.

"Yup, it was shocking," I tell her. Her words serve as a reminder that Nick and I should not be doing this. Every word she used adequately describes him. How could he think we could take on the responsibility of raising a child together? We can't.

My sister gets up from the beanbag and sits on the edge of my bed. "What else did he say?" she asks, eager to know it all.

I debate about whether I should tell her. She'll think it's a joke and laugh. It'll be ridiculous but do I want to keep it to myself? I decide to say it anyway because I can't contain it. "He asked me to marry him."

"He did what?" she says, her eyes widening.

I'm really tired of having to repeat everything. "He said we should get married."

"Why?" my sister replies.

Shrugging, I rest my head against the headboard. "I guess he thought he should propose since I'm carrying his child."

"That is..." she starts, but I interrupt.

"Funny? Stupid?"

"Unexpected," she finishes.

"Why?" Because a guy like him wouldn't want to own up to his responsibility? Because I'm not worth marrying? Because he's popular and I'm not? Is that what my sister is thinking? All these thoughts come to mind but I don't voice any of them.

"It just surprises me. Seems real mature of him. But also like something he might've meant. Unless he said it with a smile on his face," she pauses and looks to me. I shake my head, which makes her continue, "He must really like you."

"Like me? Why would you say that?" I ask.

"He wants you to keep the child, wants you guys to raise it together, and asked you to marry him. If he didn't like you, he'd be encouraging you to not have the child or tell you he wouldn't be helping. He certainly wouldn't have talked about marriage. Nick seems like the guy who wouldn't want to be tied down to anyone. And then you tell him you're pregnant and he instantly imagines a life where you're all together. A happy family."

My sister's words wash over me like a wave coming out of nowhere. Is there some truth to what she's saying? I mean, it is Nick. Nick would run for the hills before being tied down.

"Has he been seeing other people?" my sister asks the question she asked me a couple weeks ago. Why do I have to keep answering this? Why is it so hard to believe?

"He says he hasn't been," I tell her. I guess I wouldn't really be able to confirm, seeing as we don't run in the same circles.

"Yeah, I thought so," my sister says, lying on the bed now.

"What do you mean?" I ask.

"The girls on the cheerleading team... they always try and hit on him." That's the first time I hear of this from my sister, but I guess it doesn't surprise me. I'm sure a lot of girls hit on Nick.

"And?" I press, wondering where this is going.

"And he jokes around or whatever but just keeps walking. I've heard Gisele, the cheer captain, talk about how before, there used to be a lot of drama on the team because he'd basically sleep with all of them. Apparently, now he doesn't even give them the time of day. They wonder what's changed." Elia's words have two effects on me and they're opposite from each other. The first makes me upset.

Upset at the fact that he'd slept with a bunch of girls, allegedly including the entire cheerleading team.

But also, for a moment, I'm overcome with pride because maybe, just maybe, I'm the reason he's not doing that anymore. Which brings me to the next feeling. The feeling I get when I'm with him. When he kisses me softly. When he runs his fingers through my hair. The same feeling that reverberates through my body as he takes his place on my bed. As he begs me to spend the night.

*You may catch feelings*, the words from his text come rushing to the front of my mind. I told him I wouldn't but maybe I already have.

"So he must like you. Like, really like you. Maybe even love you," my sister says, and I realize I've missed whatever else she said in between.

I almost choke at the mention of the word love. "Love? Yeah, okay, let's not push it, Elia."

"He asked you to marry him," she replies.

"It's not like he got on one knee and proposed. He did it out of a sense of duty," I tell her.

My sister looks at me skeptically. "Do you really think Nick Hunter is the kind of guy who would do something he didn't want to do? Out of a duty?" she asks, and the truth of her words are like a slap on the face. I know the answer to this but I argue with it anyway because it's just not possible.

"If it weren't for the pregnancy, he wouldn't have asked," I tell her.

"Maybe not," my sister starts, and I feel deflated. "Not yet anyway," she says, and that

rekindles the hope. I'm not sure why I'm sitting here contemplating a life where he would ask me to marry him in the future.

"What did you tell him?" She asks.

"I said he was being ridiculous," I tell her.

She shrugs. "Was he though?" she asks, and it feels like I'm the only sane person here.

"Marrying him was definitely never part of the plan," I tell her. Even dating him wasn't.

"Plans change," she says, and if that isn't the God-honest truth, I don't know what is. My

plans have changed in a matter of minutes. They changed the moment I looked at the first pregnancy test and saw that it was positive. That set everything else into motion. Though maybe that wasn't where everything started to change, maybe the beginning of the end was when I started talking to Nick in the first place.

Nick changed everything.

I wasn't supposed to fall for him. Wasn't supposed to like him or want to be with him, let alone want to marry him. And now I'm faced with too many decisions. Too many emotions. And no clue how to start making them.

So, I guess it's time to bring in a professional.

# 24

## NICK

I look around Eclipse and think about whether I want to tell the rookie what's on my mind. I explained to him the whole thing about seeing Amelia today because he was going off about how great it is to be in a relationship and I just blurted it out. I also told him she's pregnant, but I'm a bit embarrassed to tell him I proposed to her. "I asked her to marry me yesterday," I say it anyway. May as well give him the entire story.

"You did what?" Lincoln asks. I take a sip of my beer and wait for the lecture I expect will come. He seems like the kind of guy who walks a straight line and will have something to say about the predicament I'm in.

"She's pregnant," I tell him.

I'm surprised he looked more shocked at me asking her to marry me than me telling him she's pregnant. "And that means you had to ask her to marry you?" he asks.

I nod. "She doesn't want to be a single mom, so yeah," I tell him.

"I'm sure that statement wasn't an invitation for a proposal," he says with a chuckle. "From what you've just told me about her, I'm sure that didn't go over well."

At this point, I've told my dad, Kaitlyn, my brother, that random police officer, and now Lincoln. I see him enough times a week that getting some advice from him wouldn't be so bad.

Lincoln bailed me out of jail. He fought the hockey guys for me too. He's not a bad guy. He's a great quarterback. I can say that now that we've played a few games. He's been nothing but trustworthy since he got here and seems knowledgeable enough that I can actually talk to him about this without him making fun of me and the whole situation.

"She turned me down," I tell him.

He laughs and I toss back the rest of my beer then signal the bartender to get me another one. "I mean, what did you expect? She'd tell you she's pregnant, you'd offer to marry her, she'd say yes, and then you guys would live happily ever after?" When he says it like that, it does sound too easy to be real.

"I don't know what I'm supposed to do. She's thinking about giving it up for adoption or having an abortion. I want her to keep it. I don't know what to do," I tell him honestly. The first thing I did in handling this whole thing was terrible. I want to make it all right.

Lincoln takes a sip of his Coke and I shake my head at him. Now that I think about it, I don't think I've ever seen him have a sip of alcohol. Maybe it's a no alcohol during the season kind of thing? "Just be there for her. Whatever she decides. Remember that this will affect her more than it will you," he says, interrupting my thoughts.

I nod. I hadn't thought about it that way. I mean, she's the one who will look visibly pregnant. The one whose body will change. The one who, if she chooses to keep it, will have to carry it around for nine months. All these thoughts come to mind while I down the rest of my beer. I'm not planning on getting drunk anytime soon, the last time was a bit of a wakeup call, but I definitely gotta have a buzz for this conversation. I can't just talk about feelings with a guy without there being some alcohol involved.

Another thought comes to mind and, before I can shut it down, I speak. "It's my kid too," I tell him. "Shouldn't what I have to say matter?" I ask.

"I'm sure it does. I'm sure she listened to what you had to say. I can assure you she's mulling it over. This isn't easy for her. It's not easy for you either but you need to understand that the ultimate choice is hers." He's right. She was listening. She told me she would take everything into consideration when making a decision.

I look at Lincoln, surprised at how much he knows. The maturity in his words is surprising for a guy who just started college. I mean, I should be ashamed that I came to an eighteen-year-old for advice. "How do you know so much?" I ask.

"Life experience," he responds, finishing his drink.

"You're only eighteen, what could you have possibly experienced?" I ask.

"More than you know," he says, and the look in his eyes shows me that this isn't something he wants to talk about. Fine by me, I've got enough problems of my own right now to force someone to tell me about theirs.

## 25

NICK

I wake up to the sound of my alarm. It's 5 am and I have to be at the gym. I don't know why going this early seems like a good idea. Oh right, because I have classes to go to too. It's hard being a football player and a scholar. Probably why my grades aren't the best. I roll out of bed and stop the alarm on my phone. The brightness feels blinding and, when my eyes finally adjust to it, I see an incoming text message from Lincoln.

Lincoln: Can you pick me up for the gym? My girlfriend took the car last night.

I realize that the message came in last night. I guess I must've fallen asleep earlier than I thought or maybe I just stopped paying attention to my phone when I realized Amelia wasn't going to be texting me any time soon. I can't blame her for it though, she has a lot on her mind. I just wish she'd talk to me about it all, let me help.

**Me:** Still need a ride?

I ask, wondering if he got one of the other guys to do it for him. I'm about to set the phone on the sink when it buzzes again.

**Lincoln:** Yeah, that'd be great.

**Me:** Okay, I'll be there in fifteen.

**Lincoln:** Don't you need my address?

**Me:** I know where you live.

**Lincoln:** I won't even ask how.

**Me:** I know everything, dude.

I figured out where he lived the moment I knew he was replacing Colton and refusing to live at the Football House. Back when I thought he was just an ass. I've learned to understand his decision over time, and it was around the same time I started seeing Amelia. I guess being at her place so often made me realize why it wouldn't be such a terrible idea to live with a girlfriend. My mind wanders but then I look at the time and begin rushing through my routine.

TWENTY-FIVE MINUTES LATER I PULL UP IN FRONT OF LINCOLN'S HOUSE. I'm about to text him when I look out the window and find him already jogging in my direction.

He reaches the car and opens the passenger door. "Why are you always late?" he asks, seemingly annoyed.

"It's too early for this, man. Just get in," I tell him. He really reminds me of my brother.

He clicks on his seatbelt. "Seriously though. You may as well not say a time of arrival if you're going to be late." I'm not sure where this is coming from.

I pull out onto the road. "I feel like, for a person I'm giving a ride to at 5 am, you should be less of a dick." I haven't had to deal with him this early, so maybe he's a worse morning person than I am.

He takes a deep breath, "Sorry," he says, his apology surprising me.

"I was kidding, dude," I tell him. He doesn't need to apologize. It's not that serious. I drive toward the gym with an uncharacteristically silent Lincoln on my right. I'm usually not good at picking up on signs but something tells me there's something wrong with him. I wonder if it has to do with the fact that his girlfriend took the car.

"Did she break up with you?" I ask, unable to hold back the question. What can I say? I like knowing things. Plus, someone else's problems would be a great distraction from my own—from having to wait for Amelia to decide.

He straightens out. "Why would you say that?" he says, his voice sounding slightly hurt, I think.

"I don't know. You look like someone kicked your dog. You're in a terrible mood and you're usually less temperamental. You also said she took your car, so I figured she may have left you and that's why you're miserable."

He sighs. "She didn't break up with me."

"Did you want her to break up with you?" I ask, looking in his direction briefly before focusing on the road ahead.

"No!" he replies.

I lift my hands defensively before placing them back on the steering wheel. "Okay, okay, relax. So, why'd she take your car," I ask, finding that it's much more fun being the one asking the questions instead of answering them.

"She went back home," he says, not sounding too happy about it.

"For good?" I ask, wondering why going back home is such a bad thing. I go there all the time. Every Sunday to be exact.

"No. She'll be back Sunday," he replies. "I should've gone with her," he adds.

He couldn't have because we have a game this weekend. So maybe that's why he's in such a piss poor mood. "You can just go with her when you don't have a game," I tell him, and by that, I mean when the football season is over.

"I know. It's just..." he says.

"What?" I ask, pulling into the parking lot.

He sighs. "I'd rather not talk about it," he replies, which just makes me even more intrigued.

Now I want to talk about it. "Wait, so I tell you about my life but you don't tell me about yours?" I ask.

"This isn't for me to talk about," he says, and I decide to stop pressing. I need my quarterback to be in a good mood if we're going to win Saturday's game. I'm not about to piss him off and get iced out. He's already not in a good mood, so I don't need to make it worse.

I decide I know the best way to get him to focus on something else. "So, should I ask Amelia to marry me again?" I ask and wait for him to tell me I'm out of my mind.


## AMELIA

I THOUGHT AND THOUGHT ABOUT HOW TO APPROACH THIS conversation for the last two weeks. I drop my backpack in a corner of the room and drop on the bed. I've tried to focus on class and think about my choices, but I can't do anything without first talking to my mom. She'll know what to do.

I've barely gotten any sleep since finding out I'm pregnant. A big part of that is that I know that talking to Mom has never been easy, and this time I'm facing the hardest conversation I've ever had to tackle. But I need her. A girl just needs her mom sometimes to guide her in the right direction. And I need guidance. I can't think of anything truer than that right now.

Sighing loudly, I decide that I need to just rip off the Band-Aid. I know my mom will be disappointed in me; I am. But I have to talk to her about it. I can't make a decision without her help, without her input.

After spending a few minutes making sure I look my best, hoping that it'll at least help me feel better, I grab my phone and stop prolonging the inevitable.

Instead of searching through the contacts, I dial my mom's number from memory. The phone rings a couple of times and I find myself hoping she doesn't pick up. To my disappointment, after the third ring my mom answers. "Hi sweetie!" she says excitedly.

"Hi, Mom!" I tell her.

"Are you home?" she asks.

"Yes, I am," I tell her. The moment the words leave my mouth the phone beeps and I realize she's calling me through Facetime. This is going to be much worse than I expected.

I take a deep breath then answer her Facetime call. On the other side, my mom looks at me with a big smile. "It's so good to see you! I feel like I've barely heard from you the last few days," she says. I wave at her with one hand while holding the phone to my face with the other.

"Sorry about that!" I tell her. I've been ignoring her phone calls. I'd send her text responses to whatever questions would come up, but I knew if I stayed on the phone with her long enough she'd figure out something was wrong. Mom always knows.

"How have you been?" she asks, and the question brings tears to my eyes. "How are classes?"

"Classes are good," I tell her. They've been kicking my butt. Partly because the classes are tough and also because my mind is elsewhere.

"And how are you, sweetie?" she asks again.

It's now or never. "I've been okay," I tell her, not really knowing how to go from a greeting to telling my mom I'm pregnant.

I try to smile but I can already tell Mom knows something isn't right. Even from afar, she gives me that knowing look. A phone conversation definitely would've been easier. At least I wouldn't have to look at the disappointment in her eyes when I told her.

"Talk to me, Amelia. What's going on?" she asks, and I see her sit down at her favorite chair. It's really old and doesn't fit with the décor of the house but it's something she refuses to get rid of. It used to be her grandmother's. I think she feels connected to her when she sits there. Grandma was the one person who was there for Mom when she needed it most.

I can't help the tear that makes its way down my cheek. "I'm sorry, Mom," I tell her and watch a worried look instantly take over her face. I decide to speak quickly before she thinks someone died or something. "I know you always say to stay away from athletes," I start.

I can't see her reaction because my eyes are closed. I can't do this while looking at her, I just can't. "Okay, so you like an athlete," she says.

I nod. "I'm..."

"You're in love with him?" she adds.

I ignore her question and then just go straight for it. No point in delaying the inevitable. "I'm pregnant." The words leave my mouth and my eyes remain closed. There's silence on the other end of the line, which causes tears to stream uncontrollably down my face.

"Amelia," my mom says, her words low.

"I'm sorry, Mom," I tell her, my eyes still closed. "I'm sorry I disappointed you. I'm sorry I didn't listen to you."

"Amelia, open your eyes and look at me," my mother orders but I can't get myself to. "Amelia King, open your eyes and look at your mother," she commands and I obey. It's the least I can do.

"I'm sorry, Mom," I tell her again. My arms feel weak and my phone feels like it weighs a ton. "I'm sorry I disappointed you."

She nods slowly and I feel her heart breaking. I wait for her to speak. To say something. To tell me how stupid I am. "I'm not disappointed in you, Amelia," she says.

"What?" I say, surprised at her response.

"I know I said no athletes. I bet you tried to not like him. To not fall for him. I know you definitely weren't trying to be pregnant. I sure wasn't," she says. My mom was pregnant with Elia and me when she was in college. She didn't finish school. She struggled. Her family shut her out. Our biological dad walked out before we were even born. He was a college student who wasn't about to be a father.

"I wasn't, Mom, I swear," I tell her.

My mom's eyes bore into me, even from a distance. "It's okay. It happens."

"But you told us to not let it, Mom. You warned us," I tell her.

"We just have to figure out what's next," she says. There's no disappointment in her voice. No hint of anger. Not even surprise. All I get from her is understanding and now more than ever I wish she were here. I wish I could melt into her embrace.

"You and your sister were the best things to ever happen to me, even under the conditions. And not all people are like your father," she says. "Look at how Diego's stepped up." My stepdad, Diego, met my mom while she was pregnant. He was still in college and noticed when my mom stopped showing up to one of the classes they shared. He asked a friend about my mom and ended up taking her the assignment sheets she had missed. Over time, he fell in love with her and has been a father to Elia and me since. They got married a year later and he went as far as formally adopting us. He's the only father we've ever known. "I don't think warning you to stay away from athletes was the right way to do it and, who knows, maybe this guy's the right one for you, circumstances aside," she says.

"I don't know that he's the right one," I tell her.

"And that's okay too." Who is this woman? Because that's not at all what I expected to hear from my mother.

"What do I do now, Mom?" I ask her, hoping she can tell me what to do. "I had plans."

"You don't have to give up your plans. You can still accomplish your goals. You don't have to take the same steps I did," she says. "You're a lot stronger than I was at your age. You will figure this out."

"I need your help, Mom," I tell her honestly.

"And I'll be here for you every step of the way, Amelia."

"I'm sorry," I say again, unable to help myself. I know that even if she doesn't show it, she has to be disappointed in me. I was supposed to do better.

"No need to say sorry, baby. We take things in stride. We modify our plans. We analyze our options and we make choices."

"I love you," I tell her, breaking down in tears once again.

"I love you too," she adds.

FOR THE NEXT TWO HOURS, MY MOM AND I TALK ABOUT EVERYTHING. I explain to her the whole ordeal with Nick, despite how embarrassing it feels. Then, Dad gets home and we tell him what's happening too. My sister comes into my room and we all sit in front of our screens and talk about everything together. Like a family. They listen to me as I talk about my options while assuring me that they'll be there no matter what. When the call ends, I feel relieved.

While the weight of my decisions is heavy, my family has shown me I won't have to carry it alone.

# 26

## AMELIA

I wake up the next day and don't feel like the world is ending, so that's progress. I give full credit to having the best mom and dad in the world. I'll even give some credit to my sister, though maybe not out loud.

Grabbing my phone from next to me, I look at the time. It's 10 am. I'm so glad I don't have class today. It's been a bit much juggling the news with attending my lectures and trying to pay attention. I look at my phone and find no incoming messages from Nick, which is understandable since I told him I needed space. Space to decide what to do next. Oddly enough, the answer, I think, is here quicker than I expected.

Mom told me whatever decision I made she'd be okay with as long as I was okay with it. I feel like I was so scared to think about disappointing her that I wanted to make it all go away.

But now I feel like there's a world of opportunity that's opened up.

I get up from the bed and stand in front of the mirror. I place my hands on my stomach. I can't believe there's something growing inside of me. I stand there and let my mind wander. I know it wasn't part of the plan, but plans change all the time. Plans are adjusted. Resilience is moving forward when things don't work the way we intended them to.

I start to think about what a child from Nick and me would be like. Then, I think about how to break the news to him. Instantly, something comes to mind. It's totally out of character, but I think that's why it'll work. Because it's unexpected. I walk out of my bedroom and straight into my sister's room.

"You forgot how to knock?" she replies the moment she sees me.

I shrug. "Just pulling a page from your book," I tell her.

"I always knock," she replies, and I notice the cheerleading uniform on her bed.

"That's because I lock my door."

"I don't even know why," she says, walking toward her closet.

"I've told you this before. An additional barrier in case someone breaks in. They'll go for you instead of me," I say and wait for her to look at me before I smile.

She rolls her eyes. "You're in a good mood."

I nod. "Yeah, who would've thought talking to Mom would make me feel better instead of worse?"

"Honestly, I swear you're the favorite. If it had been me telling her I was pregnant, I wouldn't be alive to tell the story," my sister says, with a pair of shoes in her hands, which she sets down on the ground next to the bed.

I take a seat on the edge of her bed. I don't come into this room often enough. It's bigger than mine and decorated beautifully. I probably should add a painting or two to my bedroom. "I've said this my entire life," I joke.

"Why are you in my room and so cheery at 10 am on a Friday?" she asks.

"I have made a decision about what to do," I tell her.

She sits next to me on the bed, careful to not sit on her uniform. "You have?! Already? Tell me!"

"I think the biggest block I had was telling Mom, but then yesterday's conversation really helped," I tell her.

"So, are you going to tell me or what?!" she asks, getting up from her bed.

"I wanted to tell Nick first," I tell her. "I'm going to keep it," I add.

Her eyes open wide as she looks at the pep in my step and the smile on my face. "You're keeping it?!" she exclaims.

I can't help it, I nod. "Yes!"

"I'm going to be an auntie!!" she runs around the room and shouts.

"Calm down, Elia!" I tell her.

"So, what did Nick say?!" she asks.

"I haven't told him yet," I reply, getting up from her bed and walking toward the door.

She looks at me, seemingly confused. "But you just said you wanted to tell him first..."

"Right, but then I thought of a better idea and came here so you can help me execute it," I tell her.

My sister looks at me skeptically. "You need my help with something," she says, like she's never had me ask her for help before. I mean, I guess I rarely go to her for assistance. It's usually the other way around, her coming to me.

"Yes, I do!" I tell her.

"What can I do?" she says, more than willing to assist.

## 27

NICK

"Hunter, someone's outside looking for you," Coach Wilson says and the look on his face is not a happy one. Coach hates when players aren't all in on game day. He hates interruptions. We're playing soon and distractions aren't really called for.

"Me?" I ask, wondering who it could be.

"Is there another Hunter here?" he asks, and I take that as my cue to get up from the bench. "Make sure you finish whatever business you need to finish and get your damn head in the game, son," he adds. Whoever is waiting for me outside better have something important to say. I'm sure Coach's wrath will be directed at me the remainder of the game.

I walk past the guys and make sure to avoid Coach Wilson's eyes. Walking out the door, I come face to face with Amelia. "What are you doing here?" I ask, walking right up to her. I look at her to make sure everything's okay. I haven't seen her since Tuesday, the longest four days of my life.

I want to kiss her, hug her, lift her up and spin her around, but my feet are pinned in place as I take in the foreign sight of her waiting for me outside the locker room. "You have a game," she says with a smile on her face.

"I have games most Saturdays," I tell her. "This is the first time I've seen you here. Is everything okay?" I ask. I look back at the door to make sure it's still shut. I won't lie, I'm afraid Coach's head will pop out any second and he'll yell at me in front of her.

Her eyes move from the door behind me to me. "I'm sorry. I bet you have a pre-game routine I'm interrupting right now," she says, her cheeks reddening. Is she nervous? That makes me nervous.

I look around then tentatively take hold of her hand. When she doesn't pull away, I grab the other. "Don't worry about that, are you okay?" I ask again. Amelia being at a football game is nuts. I've asked her a million times and she's always said no. Her being here with me right now is unreal and a little bit unsettling.

"I'm okay. I just wanted to tell you I made a decision," she says.

I feel my heart beating quickly, like it does right after I run a route. "You have?" I ask her nervously.

She nods. "I wanted to tell you before the game," she starts. "I talked to my parents about our situation," she says, looking down at her stomach and then back up at me.

I try not to look terrified at the thought of her talking to her parents. "That must've been a big deal. Are you okay?" I ask the same question over and over again because I don't know what else to say.

She smiles and that gives me instant relief. "It was a really great conversation. Much better than I expected. She helped me come to a decision," she says.

"And the decision you came up with was?" I ask, scared to hear her response.

She lets go of my hand and rests it on my chest instead. "I've never seen you in uniform before, and I gotta tell you, it doesn't look half bad," she jokes.

"Any other time I would take that and run. But I'm hanging on your every word, so can you please tell me what you decided?" I tell her.

"Did you mean it?" she asks.

I'm so confused right now. "Mean what?"

"Mean it when you said you were willing to try," she says, her eyes fixed on the floor.

I bring my hand under her chin and lift until her eyes meet mine. "Every word," I tell her.

She closes her eyes and takes a deep breath. "I've decided that plans sometimes change. I think I can do this. I know I can do it without you—"

"You won't need to," I tell her, interrupting her. I want her to know that I'll be there.

"I can do it without you," she finishes anyway, "but if you want to do it with me I won't stop you."

I bring my arms around her, hugging her tightly. Then, remembering she's pregnant, I pull back. "So, we're having a baby?!" I exclaim.

"Ssshhh," she says, laughing. "Yes, we're having a baby," she whispers.

Coach Wilson chooses this precise moment to walk out of the locker room. "Are you done here, Hunter? Or did you forget we have a game to play?" Coach scolds me. I'm too happy to care about being yelled at right now.

"You gotta go," Amelia says, pushing me away.

"Will you stay for the rest of the game?" I ask her.

She nods. "Elia got me a ticket. I'll be there."

"What seat?" I ask.

Coach clears his throat and I ignore him.

"I'm not really sure," she tells me.

"I'll look for you," I tell her, walking backward.

Coach clears his throat. "Coming!" I tell him. "Thank you!" I tell Amelia.

"Have a good game!" she responds.

133

I look at her then back at Coach Wilson. "I'm going to have the best game of my life," I declare. I wave to Amelia and walk past Coach and disappear into the locker room.

If guys had trouble taking me down before, just wait till they try today. I don't think anything can bring me down. Not when Amelia just gave me the best pre-game speech ever heard.

## 28

## AMELIA

I don't know a single thing about football. I don't know what anything is called, except for the quarterback. And well, I know that Nick is a tight end. I know he wears number 87. I've seen his practice jersey enough times to look at the number and he's bragged enough about being the best tight end in the game for me to remember.

But aside from that, and our school colors, I know nothing.

I sit there in a sea of people feeling out of place. A little bit uncomfortable but also at peace. It's been a crazy couple of weeks with twists and turns but I finally feel like I'm starting to make sense of things.

I'm a senior at Bragan and I really thought I could make it all four years without ever having to come to one of these games. I guess at the end of the day, if you didn't go watch a football game, did you really go to Bragan University?

. . .

I WATCH AS THE CHEERLEADERS MOVE ABOUT, TRYING TO GET THE crowd excited. I watch my sister as her ponytail bounces back and forth. She's got a smile plastered on her face and, while I always thought cheerleaders' smiles were just for show, I know my sister's is genuine. She's really happy to be a part of this. Part of the cheerleading team. She loves it. So much so that I can tell that even when she gets home she'll be smiling from ear to ear for a few more hours.

It's like a high for her.

I hope law makes me as happy as cheerleading makes her.

The announcer announces the other team that's playing, but amidst the noise, I can barely catch their name. They run through the field to a mixture of noise. The people around me are booing, but I can also hear some cheers. It must feel crappy to walk out onto the field and have people yelling at you. But I guess that's what happens in sports.

Maybe they use it to fuel them. I wouldn't know. I never did any team sports.

The moment the Bragan Lions are introduced, the people next to me stand from their seats and begin shouting. I'm sure some people are booing, but I can't hear any of it, not with how loud the praise from the crowd is.

I look around and decide to join in on the fun. I may not understand football, but the buzzing in this environment and the million things that have happened in the last week make me want to get up and scream. So I do. I mean, when else would I be able to just yell and have no one look at me like there's something wrong with me?

Elia got me a good enough seat that I can see everything on the field. I look behind me and see the masses of people. Having driven to the parking lot and never gone inside, I never imagined this to be as large as it is. The sheer number of people in this stadium confirms the one thing I've always known yet never truly grasped, the magnitude of football at Bragan University.

I look back at the field, my eyes searching for Nick, until I spot his number. I realize that this is his element. That out there on the field, to all these people, he is larger than life.

And yet he's with me.

## NICK

IT'S THE FOURTH QUARTER. THE GAME IS TIED AND WE JUST GOT BACK from the timeout following the two-minute warning.

I jog from one end of the line to another and watch who follows me. When I have him in my sights, I smile. There's no way he's going to keep up with me. No way.

I wait for Lincoln to make the call and, the moment the ball is snapped, I run. I fake left and go right, leaving the guy who was supposed to cover me in the dust.

Running the route, I turn to look at Lincoln, hoping he finds me. He does and sends a bullet my way. I catch it and just as quickly turn back around and begin to run. I'm on their forty-yard line as I see two defenders running up toward me. I lower my shoulder and run straight into the first guy, taking him down.

Losing my balance a little, it takes me a few seconds to regain my footing. I ensure that the football is held tightly in my hands, as I can't afford to lose it. I'm on their 30-yard line now and the sounds from the crowd keep propelling me forward.

This is where football is played. In the last few minutes. I keep running and dodge another defender before I'm taken down by two others.

As I lie on top of them I realize something, I haven't touched the floor yet and the refs haven't whistled, so the play is not dead. The moment the thought comes to mind, I get up and keep running.

It takes the rest of the players a moment to realize what's happening, but by that point, it's too late. I find myself quickly approaching the twenty-yard line, then the tenth.

When I'm close enough, I take a look behind and see the guys chasing after me. No way they'll reach me, so I dance my way into the end zone.

I watch as the ref lifts both hands in the air, calling it a touchdown. I focus on the announcers as I hear their confusion over what happened. I look at the opposing sideline and watch the red flag on the field as their Coach challenges the call. I mean, the touchdown would be reviewed anyway, so I'm not sure why he threw the flag. Anger makes people do crazy things; I should know.

My teammates run over to me, Lincoln surprisingly reaching me first. "What just happened?" he asks, a little winded.

"I never touched the floor," I tell him and the rest of the guys who surround me.

They pat me on the helmet. "Seriously?" Lincoln asks.

I nod. "When they took me down, I landed on top of them. I never touched the floor and neither did the ball. There was no whistle either, so the play was live."

The guys look at me in disbelief. Then, we all turn to watch the replay on the screens. They repeat the video, showing four different frames. It takes seconds for everyone to realize what I knew the entire time.

"The call on the field stands, touchdown!" The ref says and the call is followed by chants from all around the stadium. I look around and take in the familiar Hunter chants. I try to find Amelia but fail as the sea of people is too large to make her out.

Next time she comes to a game, I'll give her tickets to the suite. The best seats for the mother of my child. That feels so weird to say but I don't mind it.


I WATCH FROM THE SIDELINES AS OUR DEFENSE SACKS THEIR quarterback a third time. It's now third and twenty and the game is practically sealed. With less than ten seconds left on the clock, their offense calls a predictable Hail Mary.

Following the quarterback with my eyes, I stand on the sideline waiting for the ball to be snapped. He takes a few steps back then the ball leaves his hand. I watch the ball in the air then look around the back field for any open receivers.

Just as the ball comes down, it's batted away by one our safeties,

Ramirez, for an incomplete pass. We jump up and down in excitement when we look at the clock and notice there's no time left.

We run to the field as we celebrate yet another victory. Another game closer to the National Championship. Another game closer to winning it all.

After celebrating with my teammates for a few minutes, I turn to see the cheerleaders still hyping up the crowd. I can't help it; I walk away from my teammates and straight toward them.

The moment I approach, I pretend to do one of their dances, which makes the crowd laugh. I'm happy, really happy right now and making a fool of myself is just what I do.

The girls on the team turn to me and laugh.

Instantly, one of them breaks formation, or whatever you call it, and walks over to me. I recognize her from some of our parties. "Great game out there," she says.

"Thank you!" I reply.

She places her hand on my arm, "Are we celebrating today?" she asks, batting her eyes at me. I look at her arm and remove it from its resting place.

"I'm sure the guys are," I tell her then watch as she pouts.

I walk around her, not wanting anything to do with her. "Elia," I say, and she looks around at the other girls before walking over to me. I don't miss the envy in her teammates' eyes as she walks toward me.

"Yes?" she asks as she reaches me. I know she's not used to me talking to her in public either because I never do. Our friendship has been limited to her house. But hey, there's no reason why I can't bother her around others now.

"I like this uniform," I tell her. "Fits your personality," I add.

She rolls her eyes. "Shut up. What do you want?" she asks.

"Your sister," I tell her, and the words just roll out of my tongue. "I mean, I want to know where she is," I clarify.

"Sure you do," she says with a knowing smile. "She's over there!" she says, pointing to the side. I follow her fingers and sure enough I find Amelia standing with a smile on her face a few rows up.

"Thanks," I tell Elia without even looking at her. I'm too

distracted by Amelia and the excitement on her face. I hope she liked what she saw today because she's the reason I was unstoppable. I knew I would be from the moment I saw her.

Now, I just gotta get her to come to every game and cheer me on. She can be my personal good luck charm if she wants to.

I walk away from the cheerleaders and start jogging over to my girl. The people around her begin clapping as they see me move in their direction. She doesn't notice me until I'm standing right in front of her.

Jumping over the barrier that separates the players from the spectators, I'm instantly rushed by strangers who congratulate me.

"Thank you, thank you!" I tell them as I move through the crowd. I hear more congratulations from behind me but I don't pay them any mind.

Amelia's row is now empty with everyone moving closer to the action. I walk up the steps, leaving everyone else behind, and reach her. She watches my every step as I close the distance between us. Taking the now vacant seat next to her, I place my hand on her knee.

"So, what did you think?" I ask, trying to control the urge to kiss her.

She looks at my hand on her knee then at me. "I don't know much about football, but from what I can tell, you killed it," she says.

I smile at her. "Then you know all you need to know," I tell her.

My eyes wander to her lips then back to her eyes. "I really want to..." I start.

She doesn't need me to finish for her to know what I'm about to say. Instead, she looks up at me, then, unexpectedly, in the middle of the stadium with people around us, she brings her lips to mine.

Maybe it's because it's in public. Perhaps it's because I just had the best game of my life. Or maybe it's because she's the mother of my child, the child we'll be raising together. It could also be because she's the one initiating the kiss. But it feels like I'm kissing her for the first time. Like I was in desperate need of something she's finally giving to me. And maybe she is? Because with this kiss, it feels like she's giving me her heart.

## 29

AMELIA

I take a seat in the rocking chair in my room as I enjoy the gift Nick got me. My hands cradle my stomach protectively as I think about how ridiculous this gift is. He said he wanted to make sure I was comfortable.

We're five weeks into the pregnancy, that's what the OB said, though I didn't need her to tell me because I knew exactly when this baby was made. It's been a little over a week since I told Nick I was keeping the baby, and already he can't help but buy things he thinks I need.

Who would've thought we'd be here? Preparing for the arrival of our kid. A life the two of us are promising to raise in this world. I think we're making the right decision. None of the choices we were faced with would've been easy, but this one is the right one for me.

Smiling, I close my eyes and let my imagination take over. Ever since Nick proposed, regardless of how ridiculous it was, I can't help but let myself think about the three of us building a family.

His proposal was unnecessary, but it didn't stop it from being somewhat sweet. This playboy of a guy was willing to settle down with me for the sake of being a family. I imagine little peanut being as strong as its dad and as argumentative as I am. The thought causes the smile on my face to widen even more.

I haven't felt this joy before and I know there's a lot more to come. I didn't mean for any of this to happen. I'm not delusional in thinking it'll be easy—going to school full-time while raising a child will be impossible without constant help. My parents have agreed to be there for us every step of the way, despite the fact that we made a mistake by being careless.

I haven't met Nick's dad yet, and he hasn't met my parents, but that'll happen soon enough. We'll plan it maybe for Thanksgiving weekend. If we don't, our parents will take it upon themselves.

I sit there and think about how I ended up here. *I knew you'd fall for him*, my sister's voice echoes in my mind. She did tell me that after seeing him at our place all the time. Who knew she would be on to something? I am falling for him. Falling for the way he seems to be taking all this. He could've easily said he wanted nothing to do with it. Could've agreed to put the child up for adoption. Even an abortion would've made his issues go away. Instead, he urged me to think about doing this together. Despite the difficulties and hardship, and putting aside his reaction on the first day, Nick's maturity has shocked me.

I'm sure he's surprising a lot of people in his life right now. Those who know anyway.

**Baby Daddy:** What are you doing?

Nick got ahold of my phone after his game last weekend and changed his name from Football Player to Baby Daddy. Apparently, it was time for an upgrade. He asked me for my phone and pretended to be hurt when I showed him what he was under in my contacts. He burst out laughing as he changed what I had him saved as, laughing.

He thought it was hilarious. I asked him what he had me as and I laughed when I saw "Smart Girl" was what he had me named.

**Me:** Right now? Laughing at your name on my phone.

**Baby Daddy:** It's better than what it was! I am your baby daddy. You're carrying my baby. If you want to change it to hubby, you just have to say yes to my offer. It still stands.

Nick has brought up the proposal thing two more times since he first asked. I turn it down every time. I wouldn't want to marry someone simply because we both made a mistake. That seems careless.

Even though sometimes I like to think about the perfect family, Nick, our child, and I could be, I know that emotions are high right now. We're facing the unexpected and we don't really know how to go about it. He went from being the guy I slept with to the guy asking me to marry him after finding out I was pregnant in a matter of weeks. It's all too fast, and honestly, I still don't think it would work.

**Baby Daddy:** I see you're thinking about it. I'll wear you down soon enough ;).

I don't know how he does it but every conversation I have with Nick ends up with me smiling down at my phone. This is yet another reason why my sister thinks I'm falling in love with him.

**Me:** My answer won't change.

**Baby Daddy:** Sure it won't. Just know I'm waiting for you. If you say yes, we can elope right now.

**Me:** Did you message me to remind me about your proposal?

**Baby Daddy:** No. I was texting to see if you needed anything. Food? Ice cream? A foot rub?

**Me:** It's too early for ice cream. I have two classes today and won't finish till 7 pm. Wait... You'd rub my feet?

**Baby Daddy:** You're going to be the mother of my namesake, Nick Jr. I'd do anything for you.

**Me:** Nick Jr.? Yeah right. We don't even know what we're having and you're already thinking about naming the child after you.

**Baby Daddy:** We're having a boy. He'll be just as stubborn and handsome as I am. He'll be a great football player too. And he'll be as smart as you. We'll name him Nick. If it's a girl, we'll name her Nicole so that they're still Nic Jr. Maybe we'll have twins.

I roll my eyes.

**Me:** The doctor already told us it wasn't twins. You're ridiculous, I haven't approved either of these names. Anyway, as long as we have a healthy baby, I don't care what we have. But I'm praying they get more of my qualities than yours. I wouldn't know how to deal with another you.

**Baby Daddy:** I'm not so bad. You chose me to be your baby daddy, remember?

**Me:** Stop it! You know I didn't mean to choose to be pregnant.

**Baby Daddy:** I know, I know. So, should I come over, bring food, and give you a massage or something tonight after class?

**Me:** I'm good. I have legs that work, so I can get myself food. If I want a foot rub, I can pay for one.

**Baby Daddy:** Mine would be free ;). Can't get any better than that.

**Me:** Go away!

**Baby Daddy:** Okay, okay...But can I come over tonight?

**Me:** Why?

**Baby Daddy:** I want to read to Nick Jr. I read that they can hear you, even when they're young. I gotta bond with him.

I think Nick keeps saying we'll have a boy because he believes if he says it enough times he'll speak it into existence.

**Me:** Fine.

**Baby Daddy:** I'll bring ice cream.

**Me:** I don't need any!

**Baby Daddy:** If you don't eat it, I will.

## 30

AMELIA

"Why are we buying baby clothes right now?" I ask Nick as we walk up and down the aisle of this baby store. This is not how I expected to spend my Friday. When Nick showed up at my place today, I thought we'd hang out and watch movies. Maybe get some food delivered and just relax. Instead, he announced that we were going out. At first, I was hesitant, but then he, in true Nick fashion, convinced me to give it a try.

He refused to tell me where we were going. When we found ourselves at the Forest Pines Plaza, I imagined we'd get some ice cream or something. He's been going on and on about me wanting ice cream because I'm pregnant, so that wouldn't surprise me.

What did surprise me was stopping right in front of a children's clothing store. He looked at me with a devious smile and I automatically knew what we were in for. More shopping.

"Our baby is going to need clothes!" He says from the other aisle. I walk around to find him holding the cutest onesie ever that says, *My Daddy is my Hero.*

"That's adorable!" I tell him.

He smiles and honestly it feels blinding. I don't know what it is but I'm finding myself more and more attracted to this guy with each passing day and with each side of him I get to learn about. Not just a physical attraction, which has always been there, but an emotional one too. "Don't worry, we didn't forget about you!" he says, putting that onesie aside and showing me the one behind it, which reads: *Mom is my second favorite.*

I take the first thing I can find, which conveniently is a baby shoe, and throw it at him. "Rude!" I say, laughing.

He chuckles loudly as he picks up the shoe and puts it back in place. "I'm kidding. I'm kidding."

"Unreal!" I tell him, shaking my head. "I'm the one carrying our child! I better be the favorite parent."

"But I'm the fun one, so he'll love his dad and want to be like him. How about this, let's share the favorite spot."

"Fine," I say, rolling my eyes dramatically and not arguing about our child's gender. He's convinced we're having a boy. "But we're going to need a different onesie," I say, walking up to him and taking the one he just showed me from his hands. "Why do they even make these?" I say in mock outrage, putting the onesie back on the rack.

So at least I wasn't fully wrong. After buying entirely too many gender-neutral outfits, Nick said we should get some frozen yogurt. After we finished, we started making our way to the parking lot.

"I can't believe you bought so many things," I tell him.

He shrugs. "Only the best for our child."

"You seem oddly relaxed with this whole parenthood thing," I tell him.

He transfers the bag of clothes from his left hand to his right.

Then, almost as if it's something he does all the time, he finds my hand. Our fingers intertwine and I like the warmth of his hand on mine. "It scares me," he says, and I can hear the sincerity in his voice.

I sigh, relieved. "Thank goodness!" I exclaim.

"You're happy I'm afraid?" he questions.

I nod.

"Why?!" he asks, shocked.

I smile.

"Oh, so you're just going to smile and not answer," he says, facing me.

I look down at our joined hands then at his blue eyes looking straight at mine. "Sorry, I was enjoying this too much," I tell him.

"I can tell," he replies. "So, why are you happy I'm scared?" he asks.

"Because then it means I'm not the only one," I tell him, opting for complete honesty.

He places the bag on the floor and holds my other hand. He brings my hands up to his lips then kisses them tenderly. "In that case, I'm happy too. Because I was pretending to not be afraid because you look like you're ready for anything," he says.

I lower our hands. Then, getting up on my tippy toes, I bring my lips to his.

"What was that for?" he asks after the kiss ends.

I shrug. "I just felt like it."

Then, he kisses me. "I just felt like it too," he says. "Just so you know, you kissing me in public just gave me free reign," he says with a wink.

I shake my head.

"We've got this, you know?" he says, his face sobering.

He doesn't waver when he says those words and I believe him. "I know," I tell him. Even if it scares us. Even when we think we won't be able to do it. We have other people here for us and, at least for now, we have each other. We'll figure it out.

He picks up the bag from the floor and we resume our walk to the car. Hand in hand, like lovers as the sun sets, we move forward. We think of the future and we wait, scared and excited about what's to come.

# 31

## NICK

It's been a little over two weeks since Amelia and I went shopping together. Since she kissed me in the middle of the plaza and let me kiss her back. When she let me hold her hand as we walked, I couldn't help but think about the future—a future with her.

In a few days, our parents will finally meet for the Thanksgiving weekend. That scares the crap out of me, but they waited long enough.

I run up and down the field with the sound of the whistle. Lincoln throws the ball my way and I catch it every time then run back and do it all over again. I guess that's what happens when you're facing tough competition. We have to win. We need to keep up the championship team we've always had. Last spring, I doubted that we could go undefeated again this year, but now, more than ever, I feel like we can. I'd like us to.

I need to make sure the NFL knows I'm the player they need. I've gotta do it not just for me anymore but for my family—Amelia and my child. I know I've got enough money in my trust fund to make an NFL salary unnecessary, but I want a legacy, something I worked for. For my child. I want him to know that I made my dreams come true so that he can do the same.

Sweat drips from my forehead as I run the next route. I miss the mark and the ball falls on the ground. "What's the matter, Hunter?!" Coach Stevens asks.

"Sorry, Coach," I tell him, shaking my head and taking my position once again.

"Get your head in the game," he shouts.

"Yes sir!" I tell him.

My eyes land on Lincoln, who's shaking his head as he prepares himself to throw the ball once again. "You getting tired?" he says with a playful smile. I flick him off.

"If only it were you running instead," I tell him. "I bet you'd tired out real quick."

"Didn't you see me on Saturday? Who ran it for a 15-yard touchdown? This guy," he says, pointing at himself. Coach calls the next route and I run it.

I toss the ball back to Lincoln. "You might have run the ball in for a touchdown, but we both know I'm what they remember from that game!" I say cockily. I mean, his play set the stage, but mine? Mine sealed the victory for us.

My game just keeps getting better. Before, I played football with popularity and fame as my motivation, but now I play for more than that. This week was an away game but I'm hoping that Amelia comes to watch this week's game.

I FINALLY EXIT THE SHOWERS AND FIND EVERYONE ELSE IS GONE. I stayed there for what seemed like hours after running what felt like three marathons at practice today. The constant running back and forth wore me out. I needed the shower to help relax my muscles so that hopefully they won't ache too much later.

When I finish, I take in my surroundings and notice there's no one else left in the locker room. I guess I must've taken longer than I thought. I put on my pants and throw my shirt over my head and head to class.


## AMELIA

I MADE IT THROUGH MY CLASSES AND GOT HOME AS SOON AS I COULD. I've been feeling weird all day. I mean, I know pregnancy comes with different moods and whatnot but I just feel funky. I can't shake this off despite how much I've tried to.

"Are you feeling better?" Elia asks, letting herself into my room.

I shake my head. "Not really."

"Does something hurt?" she asks. Since I told her I was feeling off, she's been checking on me every few minutes. She wants to make sure the baby and I are okay.

My answer remains the same. "Nope."

"So, what is it?" she asks, seemingly as baffled as I am.

I shrug. "It's just a feeling... not a physical one anyway." I know my words make no sense to her.

"Do you want to watch a movie or something?" she asks, trying to distract me. I doubt that'll work but at this point, I'll try anything.

"Sure! You can go ahead and pick one and I'll join you in the living room in a second," I tell her. I get up from my rocking chair and put on some flip flops.

Walking over to the mirror, I rest both of my hands on top of it and look at myself. I look for any telltale signs that I'm pregnant. Though I'm eight weeks into my pregnancy, I don't think I'm showing yet. I wonder if people can somehow tell by looking at my face that I'm expecting. I don't think I've changed much, but my sister and Nick keep telling me I'm glowing. Mom says the same thing when she Facetimes me. She really did take it better than I expected. I can't believe she and Dad will be meeting Nick soon. I mean, they've seen

Nick on Facetime but that wasn't enough for her. I get it, if my daughter told me she were pregnant, I'd want to meet the guy too.

The dreaded feeling returns. "Alright, just shake it off," I tell myself.

"Did you say something?!" Elia yells. I'm surprised she heard that.

Turning to the open door, I shout back, "I was talking to myself!" I don't know why I yelled. If she heard me talking to myself, then I don't think I needed to do the extra work.

"Are you coming?" she asks. "Movie is about to start!" She settled on a movie pretty quickly. It usually takes us forever to decide.

"On my way! Be patient with me," I tell her. Just as I'm about to walk out of the bathroom I realize I need to use it, so I lock the door instead.

I always thought pregnant women were exaggerating when they talked about having to pee all the time, but nope, they were speaking the God-honest-truth.

# 32

## NICK

I leave class and as I step onto the quad, I get a sinking feeling. The last time I had this feeling, I found out Amelia was pregnant and reacted like an asshole. Instantly, I check my phone but see no incoming messages. Once again, I try to shake the feeling off but I can't.

Instinctively, I do the only thing that makes sense. I head over to Amelia's house to make sure she's okay.

I ARRIVE AT AMELIA'S HOUSE IN A MATTER OF MINUTES. I'VE BEEN coming to her house so often it's starting to feel like that's my permanent home and the Football House is the place I visit instead. *I guess that's what the guys in committed relationships feel*, the voice in the back of my head says and I roll my eyes. I've judged them enough and yet here I am probably in deeper than they are. I mean, I asked the girl to marry me.

I knock on Amelia's apartment door and wait impatiently for someone to answer. That bad feeling I got earlier multiples the longer I stand here. I really wish I had keys to this place.

I knock again. "Hello," I shout from outside the door, hoping someone inside hears me and opens it. "Anyone there?" I ask, knocking again.

Just as I'm considering kicking down the door, not seriously, it opens and I come face-to-face with Elia. I'm about to joke that she saw me freak out again but stop the moment I take in the look on her face. There's no smugness there, as usual, instead, I see something I recognize as pity and sadness painted all over her expression. What's happening now?

"What's wrong?" I ask, and the moment I do it's like a dam breaks and her tears begin to roll down her cheeks. I don't do well with crying women, never have, so I stand there for a second too long wondering what to do next.

She doesn't answer me but instead looks to the side, toward Amelia's room.

I'm instantly alarmed. I walk past her and in the direction of Amelia's door. The feeling that something is wrong with Amelia spreading through me with every sob from Elia I hear behind me.

When I reach her bedroom, I don't even knock. Instead, I open it and walk right in.

# 33

AMELIA

*A few hours earlier*

"Elia," I shout from the bathroom. "Elia," I shout again and again. Holding back my tears as I look down.

"What's up?" my sister asks from the other side of the door. I shouldn't have locked it.

"Call an ambulance," I tell her. That's all I manage to say as I look down at the blood in the toilet bowl. I'm instantly hit with cramps and the pain is unlike anything I've ever experienced.

"Are you okay?" she asks, and I can hear the panic in her voice.

"Call an ambulance!" I yell again. It's going to be okay. It'll be okay, I say out loud, talking to my baby. I know Nick says they can hear you even this early. I want to comfort him or her. I want to make sure he or she knows that everything's going to be okay.

I unlock the door as soon as I can and come face to face with my sister.

"They want to know what's going on," she says, looking at me with fear in her eyes as she tries to figure out what's happening.

I cradle my stomach. "It hurts a lot. And there's blood. A lot of blood," I tell her. She repeats my words to the person on the other end of the line.

"She's pregnant," she says, giving the responder context.

"It's going to be okay," I say out loud to myself, closing my eyes as I try and believe that statement. If I don't believe it, how will my baby? I gotta believe it.


My sister manages to help me get to the living room. Then, slowly, we make our way out the door and downstairs. She tells me to just wait for them here, but I want to make sure they see me as soon as they arrive. I want to make sure they can take care of my baby as quickly as possible.

My sister looks at me with fear in her eyes as I sit there distracted by the piercing pain in my abdomen. I try not to think about how it feels like I'm still bleeding. How I may still be bleeding. But it's hard not to.

Please be okay, baby. *Please*, I plead in my head.

I know at first I didn't know what to do, but I promise you I'll be a good mom.

I promise I'll be there for you.

I'll love you with everything I have.

I already do.

Seconds later, I hear the sirens. My sister places her arm around me as she guides me out the door. I hear her words as she utters, "Please be okay, peanut." It's not until I hear the fear in her words that I realize that my own fear is legitimate.

## 34

NICK

When I open the door, I find her lying in her bed with her blanket covering everything but her face. I see the tears rolling down her face and I feel my legs weaken.

When she lays her eyes on mine, she begins to sob. Her cries get louder and louder and my legs feel heavier and heavier. But then her cries spring me to action. I will my feet to move and seconds later, I'm sitting on the bed next to her.

She rises from her position just enough so we're at eye level. A tear slides down my face before she even speaks. She opens and closes her mouth a few times to say something but no words come out. The tears though, those don't stop coming. They intensify with every second that passes and I want nothing more than to make everything okay. I'd give anything to see her smile. She breaks eye contact with me and finally speaks, "I lost him," she tells me.

I may not be the smartest person but she doesn't need to say anything else for me to understand what's happening. I've read enough books about this too—a miscarriage.

We embrace each other while she cries on my shoulder and I can't help but cry with her.

Amelia falls apart in my arms and I fall apart right alongside her.

We lost him.

We lost our baby.

# 35

AMELIA

I wake up feeling the same as I have the last couple of days. I'm by myself in my room. No Nick. I told him I needed some space. Told him I needed to be alone.

The truth is, I don't deserve his comforting.

It's my fault.

I know it is.

I lie in my bed and hug the pillow as tightly as I can.

My mind can't help but think about the million things I did wrong. The ways in which I caused this.

Maybe I stressed out too much.

Maybe I didn't take things slowly.

I should've been more calm.

Maybe I should've gone to the hospital more often.

Maybe I should've gone to the hospital earlier.

I should've gone as soon as I felt off.

Maybe if I hadn't waited so long to call an ambulance, my baby would still be here.

Maybe it's because I wished I was never pregnant in the first place when I first found out. Maybe that's why this happened, some sort of punishment.

Cruel.

That's what this is.

*"When it's too early to know the gender, we tell the parents to go with what they feel"* The doctor said to me. I don't know if she thought that would make me feel better because it didn't. Still, I think Nick and I were going to have a boy.

It's cruel to take away a child from me after I fell in love with him. After I finally started to feel like a mom. After I dreamed of a future with him.

I get up from the bed, grab the baby clothes from the top drawers in my dresser, then open the door. I throw it all across the room and into the hall then slam the door shut.

Walking back to my bed, I cover myself up with the blanket from head to toe. Maybe this is what I deserve for even considering not having him. For thinking about giving him up for adoption. For considering an abortion. Maybe he was taken away from me so this way I have no choice.

I failed. I couldn't keep my child safe. They say the womb is like a lockbox, but I couldn't protect my child in there.

How was I supposed to protect him when he arrived in this cruel world?

I may think I have all the answers, but would I have raised him right?

No point in asking all these questions when I won't have a chance to figure out the answers. I won't have a chance to fail him.

I hear a knock at the door. I ignore it, hoping my sister gets the clue and walks away.

I haven't told anyone else what's happened. The only people who know are Elia and Nick. I told Elia to not tell anyone else. I'm sure Nick hasn't either.

I barely got the chance to tell him. I wonder if he's mad that I didn't call him when I started feeling off. That I didn't tell him when I was headed to the hospital. That I didn't bother to call when I left the hospital with my heart broken into a million little pieces and my baby—our baby— gone.

I wonder if he cares. As soon as the thought comes to mind, I push it out of my head. Of course he cares. I could hear it in the brokenness of his voice. In the quiet tears he spilled when I told him. The way his body shook when he found out our baby didn't make it.

Of course he cares. Cared.

I bet he blames me too.

Even though he tried to comfort me.

I bet he judges me.

It's my fault after all.

Another knock at the door. I'm about to scream at my sister to leave me alone but then I hear Nick's voice. "I'm still here," He says from the other side of the door. I guess he hasn't left. I'm sure soon enough he will. Just gotta give it time.

He'll leave.

If I were him... I would leave me too.


NICK


"I SHOULD GO TALK TO HER," I TELL ELIA AS I LOOK AT THE BABY clothes on the floor. I wish I hadn't gotten those to begin with.

Elia picks it all up and takes it into her room. "You should give her time," Elia says,

returning and sitting on the couch next to me.

"I just need her to know I'm here," I tell her. "She's been locked in there for three days." We keep putting food outside the door to find it barely eaten. I've had to stop myself from rushing to her every time I hear her door open. Elia says I need to give her space but that's not what I want to do. I want to throw open her door and hug her. I want her in my arms. I want to comfort her.

But that's the problem, isn't it? It's not about what I want. It's about what she needs. "Maybe she needs me?" I say out loud, trying to convince Elia. She wouldn't be able to stop the Nick of before from doing whatever he wanted, but I'm trying to listen to reason. I'm trying to do the right thing.

"How are you?" She asks, and her question throws me.

"Who cares how I am? Amelia is what matters," I reply.

She nods. "You've been sleeping on this couch for days. You've missed classes and practice."

Lincoln texted me about missing everything too. I explained to him what happened. "I told one of my friends. I'm sure he'll cover for me. Not that it matters anyway," I tell her, feeling the anger start bubbling up within me. "None of those things are important."

Elia gets up and walks over to me. She takes a seat next to me. "You lost a child too." She says, bringing her hand to my shoulder. My anger dissipates, replaced by a sense of loss I don't want to feel. A feeling I've tried to push away. Bury it so deeply inside that hopefully it disappears.

"I'll be fine as long as she's fine." I get up from the couch and start pacing back and forth.

Finally deciding enough is enough, I walk down the hall and toward Amelia's room.

I close my eyes and think about whether I should be doing this. We're supposed to be a

team. I should be there for her. I should at least try.

With that in mind, I knock on her door slowly. Hearing nothing, I knock again.

Maybe she needs more time away from me but I want nothing more than to be with her right now. I lean my forehead on the door, aching to be near her. To take away her pain.

"I'm still here," I tell her. "Take as long as you need. I'll be here the whole time." I'm not sure if she's hearing me but I say the words anyway. Because I want her to know. Because I need her to know.

# 36

## AMELIA

I wake up the next day and I feel like I've lost track of time. I have locked myself in my room, only going out when absolutely necessary. Usually doing my best to avoid seeing any of them.

Locking myself in.

Making no noise.

Pretending I'm not even here.

Wishing I weren't.

And in a way, I'm not.

Crazy how something that seemed so remote a couple of months ago could become the center of your life so quickly and then destroy everything in its path.

Someone knocks at my door and I sigh in frustration. "Leave me alone!" I scream.

"Sweetie, let me in," the voice on the other side of the door says.

I spring out of bed, run toward the door and unlock it. "Mom," as soon as those words leave my mouth I throw myself in my mother's arms and begin to cry again.

"It's okay, sweetie," she responds. My legs give out from under me and I find myself on the floor. Crying. Sobbing. My mother comes down to my level. "It's okay. Mama's here. I've got you."

Her words are exactly what I didn't know I needed. I embrace her. Hugging her tightly. "I'm sorry, Mom. It's my fault," I tell her the words that have been running over my head since it happened. "It's all my fault," I say again.

"I've got her," Mom says, and I don't have to open my eyes to know my sister and Nick are the ones checking, wondering, asking if Mom needs help. I keep my eyes closed, not wanting to see them. Not wanting them to see me.

When I hear their footsteps retreat, I open my eyes and look at my mother, the strongest person I know, looking back at me. Tears pool in her eyes. "Come here," my mother says, picking me up from the floor. She closes my bedroom door and leads me to the bed.

She sits at the head of the bed, then pulls me into her arms. I crumble in her hold. I fall apart while my mother plays with my hair and tells me everything's going to be okay.

"It's my fault," I say again and again in between cries.

"It's not your fault, sweetie. It's not," she tells me and, more than anything, I want to believe her.

I CRY IN MY MOTHER'S ARMS FOR WHAT COULD HAVE BEEN HOURS. I cried so much I didn't realize when I fell asleep. When I wake up, she's still there. Holding me. Caressing my hair. I'm comforted by her touch. By her love. By her silent support.

"Thank you for being here," I tell her, looking up at her. I've looked up to her my whole life.

She gives me a loving smile. "You know I'll always be here for you. Dad was going to come since he had already taken the time off but I told him to hold off. Sometimes a girl just needs her mom," my mother says, and I remember having the exact same thought back when I was telling her I was pregnant.

"I never expected this to happen," I tell her. And I mean it. I never expected any of this to happen.

She nods. "This is something you can't prepare yourself for. But it's something you can move forward with," she says.

How can I move forward? "I don't know how, Mom."

"It starts by crying. By being angry. By being sad. By yelling. By feeling like shit. By reminiscing. By thinking about what could've been," she says.

I've felt all of those emotions every day since finding out we lost him. Sometimes I feel them all at once.

"But it doesn't end there..." she adds. "You also have to pick yourself up every day. You have to understand that it's not your fault. You have to know that this is not the end. You'll feel the loss forever but you'll learn to live with it in a way where it won't hurt as much."

"Right now I can't imagine this not hurting," I tell her.

She runs her fingers through my hair as I reposition myself to lie on her lap. "It won't happen quickly. But it's something you have to decide to move toward every single day," she says. "You've been mourning for a week now," she says, and I didn't realize that's how long it had been. Every day seems to have merged in with the next. Everything feels meaningless.

"That's not enough time," I tell her, feeling there's no escaping this feeling.

"Not at all. But you've given yourself the opportunity to fall apart. Now you gotta give yourself the opportunity to start slowly picking yourself back up."

How can she expect me to move on after a week? To pick myself back up? To think about school or anything else beyond this moment. Beyond this loss. "I can't," I tell her.

"You have to," she replies. "But it won't happen overnight. It starts with every little step. Every small decision. It starts with letting others in and not suffering on your own."

I instantly look toward the closed door knowing that Elia and

Nick stand on the other side of it. Despite how much I've pushed them away these last few days, neither of them have left me. They still check in on me. Still put food outside for me to eat. Still leave glasses of water for me to drink. They still knock at the door knowing I won't answer.

"It hurts so bad," I tell her, crying again. Part of me hopes my tears will dry up so I can't cry anymore.

My mom places her arm around me. "I know, baby. But you don't have to carry the pain alone either. We've got you. Me, your dad, your sister, and that young man out there... we've got you."

I take a deep breath and take in my mother's words. This is a process. Healing won't happen right away. The hurt won't go away. But maybe, just maybe, it'll hurt a little less eventually. "Where do I start? How do I start to feel better?" I ask her, hoping she has answers.

"It starts by putting one foot in front of the other. Even if slowly. Even if they'll be wobbly at first. It starts by deciding to take the step," she says.

I nod. I sit up straight and wipe the tears from my eyes. "What step do I start with?" I ask, determined to do something, anything, to feel better, if only by a little. To hurt less. To feel less.

"How about we get you into the shower?" my mother says jokingly, and I smile through the tears. The first smile in what feels like forever.

I nod. "Can you come with me?" I ask.

"Absolutely, Amelia. I'm here for whatever you need for as long as you need."

I hug her. "Thank you, Mom." I don't know what I would do without her.

She kisses my cheek. "Let's go take that first step."

## 37

NICK

"I don't want to go," I tell Elia for the millionth time as we walk out of her apartment. She's trying to force to go to practice for the first time this week. I'd happily sit out this weekend's game.

She turns back to look at me. "I understand that, but you have to."

"I should be inside with her," I tell her. It feels wrong to leave Amelia when she's going through so much. When she's hurting so badly, especially to go play a game.

"Mom is here; she's got her for now," Elia repeats to me for the sixth time today. I know Amelia's mom is here. She was supposed to come this weekend for Thanksgiving dinner. Their family was going to do something on their own first and then both of our families would have dinner together on Sunday. Amelia's parents were supposed to meet my dad, sister, and me. This was supposed to be a weekend of celebration and instead, Amelia's mom had to come comfort her.

Amelia sure as hell didn't need me or Elia. She refused to talk to either of us, so we needed to bring in someone else.

Her mother has helped.

Seriously helped.

I heard her voice waver the moment Elia told her on the phone. Saw the saddened look in her eyes as she walked into the apartment. She even gave me a hug, a real hug. It was unexpected. So yeah, I get it, her mom is here. But I should be there too.

"I shouldn't be going to practice right now," I tell her again. I haven't gone anywhere since we got the news. Just been on the couch waiting to be useful. Lincoln offered to bring me some clothes from my room and I took him up on the offer. I needed to be in the same place as Amelia, even if not exactly next to her.

Elia grabs me by the arm and pulls me toward the parking lot. "I need a ride to practice too," she says. This is her first practice back too.

"You have the car, you know!" I tell her, knowing whatever she says is just an excuse.

She doesn't relent. She continues to drag me toward my car. For a petite woman, she's got a lot of strength. "You need this. Trust me," she says.

I sigh loudly. "I'll go today," I tell her, giving in. I need a distraction. One that doesn't involve alcohol or fighting. Amelia would frown at that.

"Thank you!" she exclaims.

We reach my car. "This is your car?" she asks.

I nod. "Yeah, why?"

"Fancy," she responds, then rounds the car and gets in the passenger seat.

Turning on the car, I pull out of the parking lot and toward the stadium. Even though I've only missed a couple of practices, it's going to feel weird being back in the building. I don't think I've ever missed a practice before. I've been super late due to hangovers but that's about it.

I hope Lincoln didn't tell anyone else about what's going on. He told me he would only tell Coach Wilson. I just hope Coach didn't share it with the rest of the guys. Though I bet they're wondering why I haven't been at the Football House in days or why I've missed practice.

I'm sure they'll have questions. I'm sure they'll feel like I've let the team down.

But that's not the team I'm worried about.

WE REACH THE PARKING LOT OF THE STADIUM. "THANK YOU," ELIA SAYS, getting out of my car.

I unbuckle my seatbelt and step out. As Elia runs into the building, I see the guys gathered near the front door and make my way toward them.

"Look who decided to show up to practice!" one of the guys says.

Someone else whistles. "Bout time you showed up!"

"I told you guys he had to go back home, cut him some slack. It's not like he's missed a game yet!" Lincoln says, cutting through. He throws his arm over my shoulder and leads me inside the locker room.

"Close enough," one of the guys shouts but I ignore it. I'm not really in the mood to argue with anyone, let alone justify my absence. It's none of their business.

Though I guess if I were in their shoes and one of our players had to go home out of nowhere, one of our best players, I would be concerned too. I would be more than concerned, I'd be an asshole to them.

"How are you doing?" Lincoln asks the moment we're far away from the guys and no one else can hear.

I hate that question, so I shrug.

"Got it. Okay. Well, I'm here if you need to talk or anything," he says. I guess I've given him the idea that I talk about what I'm going through. That I talk about what I'm feeling, how I'm feeling. He takes my silence as a sign to keep talking. "So, I explained to Coach Wilson what happened. I told him you didn't want anyone to know. We basically told the guys you had an emergency and had to go home," he says, letting me know the cover story.

I nod. "Thanks," I tell him.

"When you go out to practice, ignore the guys' questions. Just go out there and leave it out on the field. I know it's only practice, but trust me, it'll help," Lincoln advises. I know he's been through a lot, but what would he know about this? About what Amelia is going through.

"Got it," I tell him then walk ahead of him and into the locker room. Opening my locker, I go through the motions of changing into my workout clothes; luckily, I always keep a spare here.

I go out to the field before the guys even enter the locker room. I want to make sure I don't give them the time to ask me a million questions, to make jokes, to talk to me. I'm not here for that. Honestly, I don't know why I'm here.

I should be home with Amelia. At Amelia's home. Even if she doesn't talk to me. Even if she ignores me. Even if I just sit on the couch and wonder how she's doing.

Maybe that's exactly why I need to be here right now. Maybe I need to focus my attention on something else and give her the space she needs.

---

I LEAVE PRACTICE FEELING EMOTIONALLY EXHAUSTED. I'M NOT SURE IF I've ever walked out of the locker room so quickly in my life.

Coach Wilson gave me a look of sympathy when he saw me out there. Then, I joined the quarterbacks and the other tight ends on the team and did some work with them. I didn't realize how out of shape I would feel, even though it's only been a couple of days. Every route I ran I felt as though I was carrying weights on my feet. Still, I'd done my best to avoid deep conversations and to pretend to listen to my teammates. I tried to be the Nick they know. The one who doesn't take anyone seriously. The one who's always cocky on and off the field.

I tried to give them what they expect from me but it wasn't easy. It didn't feel real, but I didn't want to feel anything anyway. I almost did something stupid too.

If it wasn't for Coach Stevens getting in the middle, Mersier would've caught a fist to the face. For a backup quarterback who never plays, he sure tried to run his mouth today about my absence. I wasn't up for that. Luckily for him, Coach Stevens and Lincoln got in the way before I got in his face.

Walking out onto the parking lot, I find Elia waiting by my car. "Have you been out here long?" I ask.

"A little under an hour," she replies.

That's a long time. "Sorry!" I tell her.

"It's not your fault. Well, it kind of is. If I didn't have to force you to go to practice today, I could've driven myself and been home a long time ago," she says.

I unlock the car and she gets in. I pull out of the parking lot quickly and head toward Amelia.

"I could've skipped practice," I tell her.

I can feel her staring at the side of my face. "But I bet it felt good to be out there on the field."

I don't know about good. "It was a distraction," I tell her. I feel exhausted now. So exhausted that I'll probably hit the couch and fall asleep instantly. It may even feel comfortable tonight.

JUST AS WE'RE ABOUT TO REACH THE PARKING LOT, MY PHONE RINGS. I look at the caller ID on the dashboard and see it's a call from Dad.

I look at Elia, wondering if she'd mind if I pick up the call. "Hi, Dad," I say, answering after Elia tells me she doesn't mind.

"Hi son, how are you?" he asks the million-dollar question. "Are we all still doing dinner on Sunday?" he asks. Damn, I forgot to tell him.

"No," I tell him.

Reaching the parking lot, I find an empty space and park the car. "How come? I thought I was finally going to get to meet the mother of my grandchild and her parents," he says, disappointed. Elia turns to look at me instantly. She's surprised I haven't told him yet.

"I'll be out there," she mouths, giving me some privacy.

I nod.

"Dad, there's something I need to tell you," I tell him the moment Elia closes the passenger side door.

"What's going on, son?" he asks. Every time he says *son*, I can't help but think of mine.

I sigh. "We're not having a baby anymore," I tell him.

"Oh," he says. "What happened?"

I close my eyes. "A miscarriage," I tell him.

"What do you need?" he asks. I was expecting him to ask me how I'm doing.

I lean back on the driver side. "I don't need anything right now. I just need Amelia to be okay," I tell him.

"I understand. But you need to be okay too," he says. "You can come home if you want to, if you need to," he tells me.

I transfer the call from the car to my phone and take the key out of the ignition. "I need to be here with her."

"Okay, son," he says that word again. "I love you," he adds.

"Love you too, I gotta go," I tell him then hang up before he has a chance to respond.

# 38

AMELIA

I shoot Nick a text message telling him to come in the room and seconds later I hear a knock at the door. "Come in," I say.

Nick's head pops in through the door. I bet he's surprised I didn't yell at him to leave me alone this time. I'm so grateful to him. He and Elia were the ones who called Mom and told her everything. She left a few minutes ago since she has to work tomorrow but promised I could call her any time and if I needed anything she'd be here.

Nick walks inside, closing the door behind him, and just stands there. I bet it's strange for him to see me. It feels like I haven't seen him in forever, though I know he's been crashing on my couch.

"Do you need anything?" he asks.

I pat the bed. "Sit here," I tell him.

He walks over to me, his steps tentative. "I feel like I'm in trouble," he says, half-jokingly.

I smile and, when I do, I see his eyes light up, temporarily replacing the pain. He smiles at me too. "Remember that time you told me you were scared about having a baby and I laughed at you?" I ask him.

He looks at me a bit confused. I know he doesn't know where I'm going with this. "Yeah," he says.

"Remember why I laughed?" I ask him.

He nods. "Because you were feeling the same way, so you were glad you got to feel that with me," he tells me, recalling my emotions exactly.

"Talk to me," I tell him, my words coming out in a half-whisper.

I see realization dawn in his eyes. Still, he doesn't give in. "What do you want me to say?"

"How do you feel?" I ask him. "How are you?" I press. Lately, it's been all about me, and maybe that was selfish but I couldn't help it. I couldn't pour from an empty cup. Couldn't give him comfort when I had none to give.

Couldn't give him strength when I was at my weakest.

I'm not okay, far from it. But I know he isn't either. Even if he looks like he's fine. "That doesn't matter. Only you matter," he says, bringing his hands to my cheek.

I place my hand on his and make sure I look him straight in the eyes. "You're allowed to feel too," I tell him.

"Where's your mom?" he asks, changing the topic.

I let him have a moment before I press again. "She left earlier today," I tell him. "Had to go back to work," I add.

"Will you be okay without her?" he asks, concern evident in his eyes.

I bring my hand to his cheek this time so we're each holding each other. "I'll be okay." Not perfect. Not whole. But slowly I'll get there.

"Good," he says.

As I watch him sitting on the bed in front of me, a million thoughts run through my head. I'm consumed by emotions. Yes, the feeling of loss is there but also a different feeling too. I spent so much time trying not to fall for this very guy in front of me. And yet here I find myself wanting to be with him. Wanting to be in his arms. Wanting to face everything that comes our way together.

"Nick," I start.

"Yes?" he asks.

"How are you?" I ask again.

He sighs. "If you're okay, I'm okay," he says. And I've never seen a more selfless person. I can tell in his eyes that he's hurting too. The light that I can usually find there is absent. Instead, there are bags under his eyes. And for some reason, he doesn't feel like his pain is worth sharing. I can see that he's trying to be strong. Trying to put me first. That's what he's done every second of this.

I know he was skipping practices and classes as he sat on my couch day in and day out waiting. My sister told me they also lost a game for the first time this season, this past weekend, breaking their status as undefeated. She didn't elaborate, but it was evident that Nick was having a bad game and without him things fell apart.

"I wish you'd talk to me," I tell him.

He drops his hand and I drop mine. We sit there staring at each other, two forces battling. "I'm glad you're doing better," he says.

"Forget about me," I start.

"I could never," He adds, interrupting me.

I smile at him. Then, as a tear slides down my face, I bring my lips to his. I kiss him softly. It's not until we stop kissing and his forehead leans on mine that I open my eyes to find tears sliding down his face.

This is the second time I've ever seen him cry; the first being when I told him what had happened. "It's okay to feel it," I tell him.

"I'm supposed to be strong," he says, his words low as if he were ashamed.

I rest my arms on his shoulders. "You've been stronger than anyone had expected. You've carried this, and me, throughout this. You've been there for me every moment," I tell him. "Let me be there for you."

He doesn't say anything and I can tell he's fighting against the tears. But he can't help them, much like I couldn't. It's like the lid that was holding back his emotions breaks open. His emotions lay on the surface and he buries his head on my shoulders.

I hear him sob and I bring my arms around him, holding him tightly. Supporting him through this like he supported me.

"I'm here for you," I tell him the words he told me through the door. The words that, while I didn't realize at the time, meant so much to me.

"We lost our baby," he says, and much like the first time, the day everything changed, we hold each other while crying.

In my arms, I feel this giant man crumble into pieces. The pain he's been carrying on his own becomes too heavy for him to bear. While I may not be able to carry his weight on my own, we can both share it. Share the pain. Share the joy.

"We lost him," he said again and again. And each utterance of that reality hurt.

WE STAYED THERE FOR HOURS. NICK CRIED LIKE I'D NEVER SEEN A MAN cry before. He had so much pain. He hurt so badly, like I did. I never expected it because, to me, I was the one who was carrying this child. The one who had this unique bond. But Nick did too. I could see it when we bought baby clothes. Every time he joked about naming our son after himself. Every time he talked about us being a family.

And I could see it today in every tear he shed. I held him while he cried until he fell asleep, like my mother had done to me this past week. And for the first time in a while, Nick and I slept in my bed. We held on for each other the whole night like we were each other's life-lines. Like we were the only ones who understood, and we kind of were. At that very moment, we shared something ugly and beautiful. Something that had the potential to destroy us but wasn't going to. Because we could do this together.

At least tonight, that's what it felt like.

Tonight, in sharing in this loss, I realized that this man who entered my life unexpectedly, went from someone I barely knew to the man I wanted to be with the most.

Tonight, it felt like we could give each other strength.

We could help each other heal.

We could do this together too.

Maybe tomorrow we'll wake up and everything will be different, but tonight, it's us against all odds. Us against all the hurt and pain and suffering. Us against the world.

# 39

## AMELIA

It's been a week since Mom left. I've decided to put one foot in front of the other. I went back to class and even went to study group. It helped catch me up on what I had missed. I've been studying for final exams like crazy. I took my second one yesterday and have two more left before I'm done. Honestly, most of the time it feels like I'm not really present. Like I'm just going through the motions. Still, I'm determined to do whatever I can to move forward. To start healing.

Tonight we're taking the night off and celebrating being halfway done through final exams by watching a movie. I'm sitting in the living room waiting for my sister to leave her bedroom and Nick to finish showering.

I think about how Nick went from someone who wasn't allowed to spend the night to sleeping in my bed every day. I don't mind it one bit.

He goes to practice and comes back. That's been his routine. I've cried less. Not a lot less but definitely less than what I used to.

Nick's been opening up to me too about what he's feeling. He's been letting me in more and more.

I search through the TV guide trying to figure out what'll hold my attention. If Nick weren't in the shower, washing off the sweat from practice, he would've already landed on something to watch by now.

"Did you find a movie?" He asks, exiting the bathroom. I can't help but look at him. He looks a lot better now and not just because he has nothing but a towel on. What stands out to me is the lack of bags under his eyes. Though there's sadness in his eyes, I know it's not swallowing him whole. Neither of us are drowning because we're keeping each other afloat.

"Yes!" I lie, knowing if I say I haven't he'll shake his head at me. I'm indecisive when it comes to this. It's a lot of pressure to choose something we'll all like.

Nick disappears into my bedroom. "I'm cominggggg," my sister yells from hers just as he disappears from my sight.

Just as Elia steps out of her room, there's a knock at our front door.

She looks at me and I fix my eyes on her, each of us silently asking the same question: who is it? In an odd display of twin telepathy, we both look down the hall toward my room. Usually, Nick is the one knocking at our door. We should just give him a key, but he's in here. So, who's out there?

Crazy that the thought of giving Nick a key doesn't revolt me. Doesn't scare me. Doesn't have me running or pushing him away. I'm letting him in more and more each day. Not just into my bed but into my heart.

The knock interrupts my thoughts, reminding me someone is waiting on the other side. I signal at my sister to get the door. She rolls her head at me but moves forward.

She opens the door without bothering to look at who it is first. "I'm looking for Nick," someone's voice booms.

"Ah, wait, are you..." My sister starts, but before she has a chance to finish her question, the guy just walks right past her and into the house.

I look at the man who now finds himself in our living room. "You must be Amelia," he says when he sees me sitting on the couch.

He's tall, muscular, and with grey eyes that pull you in and scare you at the same time. "I am," I say nervously. Can you blame me? There's a burly stranger in my living room. A stranger who knows my name.

"I'm looking for my brother," he says.

"Colton," I hear Nick's voice. I turn to find him standing on the other side of the hall. I look back and forth between the two of them. I guess the stranger isn't a stranger after all. It's Colton Hunter. Nick's older brother. The one I've heard him talk about with pride in his eyes more times than I can count.

Looking between the two of them, I realize that they too look nothing alike. I mean, yeah they have athletic, larger than life bodies but that's where it stops.

I fix my eyes on Nick and watch the smile that takes over. He basically runs the distance across the room and throws his arms around his brother.

Colton hugs him back and I can see the love they share. I look behind them at my sister, who's still standing there awestruck. I get it. Colton is in the NFL, handsome, and standing in our living room.

I let out a smile because I know how much Nick misses his brother. Even if he doesn't say it out loud, I can tell with every story he shares. Every complaint he makes about the team or the things his brother used to do that now fall on his shoulders.

I'm happy because it seems that when Nick needed it the most, his brother showed up for him. Just like my mom and sister showed up for me. Just like Nick showed up for me.


NICK


"I can't believe you're here," I tell Colton. I figured he'd be in

New York City, not at Amelia's place. I don't let go yet because, even though I saw him a couple of weeks ago, it feels like I never get to spend time with my brother anymore. I mean, I saw that coming when he got drafted but still.

"You needed me," Colton says, just like that. My big brother. I wouldn't tell him this, but man, do I look up to him.

I step back, letting go of him. "Dad told you?" I ask him.

He nods.

"Thank you for being here," I tell him. "That's Amelia," I say, pointing at her sitting on the couch.

My brother nods at her. It's Colton, so I didn't expect any more. "I know," he tells me. In a surprising move, he walks over toward where Amelia is seated, extends his hand, and shakes hers. "I'm Colton. Sorry to barge in," he says, and wow am I shocked by him. He greeted her with more than a nod and apologized in the same sentence. Mia must really be getting to him.

"That's Elia," I tell him, pointing at Elia who's still standing by the door. She walks over toward Amelia, waving at Colton in the process. He sends a nod her way too and I figured he's run out of formalities. I smile, knowing the Colton I've always known is still in there somewhere.

"Do you mind going for a drive with me?" He asks, coming over to stand in front of me.

I look at him then at the girls. "I'm supposed to watch a movie with my girlfriend and her sister," I tell him. Before I realize the words that leave my mouth, I turn to look at Amelia, waiting for her to say something. To give me some sign that I've messed up.

Instead, I watch as she smiles at me and her cheeks redden.

Wow.

"So, she's your girlfriend and I'm just her sister?" Elia says, breaking a little bit of the tension in the room, and I laugh.

"You're my friend too... eventually my sister-in-law," I joke and watch Elia roll her eyes. It feels so nice to make a joke, to laugh, to be here right now and not be sad or angry, even if only for a few minutes. "Who would've thought I'd be dating a twin as a twin?" I turn to Colton and ask.

"Your brother came all this way to see you, we can always do movie night later tonight or whenever," Amelia says.

"See, your girl approves. Your brother did come all this way on his day off to hang out with you," Colton says. Since when does he talk so much in public? He must be really worried about me.

I look at Amelia. "Are you sure?" I ask.

She nods. "Yeah, go hang out with your brother. I'll stay here and hang out with my sister."

"Don't sound so excited," Elia says jokingly.

Amelia turns to look at her. "I am excited to spend time with you, little sis!" she teases.

"Alright, well... I guess I'm going on with you. Let me go grab my wallet and shoes," I tell him. Then I turn around and walk back toward Amelia's room.

I PUT ON MY SHOES AS QUICKLY AS I CAN. TAKING A JACKET FROM THE beanbag on the floor, I step out of the bedroom and walk down the hall to the living room.

Just as I reach the others, I see my brother standing there awkwardly. "Can I ask you a question?" Elia says.

He turns to look at her and I stop myself from laughing at how uncomfortable he looks. "Shoot," he says. I cross my arms and wait.

"How did you know I wasn't Amelia?" Elia asks.

Colton looks at her then at Amelia, who's sitting there quietly watching the exchange, just like I am. "It's obvious," my brother says. Then, he sees me and calls me over. "Great meeting you," he says, then turns around and walks out the door.

I follow behind him, turning back briefly to see the look of confusion on Amelia and Elia's faces. Just as I reach the door, I decide to turn around. I run back toward Amelia and place a kiss on her lips. "I'll see you tonight," I tell her.

"Gah, I liked you guys better when you weren't doing all this in front of me," Elia jokes. I give her a hug, then walk out and join my brother who's waiting in front of the elevator.

"What did you mean it was obvious?" I ask the question that I'm sure Elia and Amelia wanted to know the answer to.

He looks at me for a few seconds. "Elia is the kind of girl you'd typically go for," he starts. The elevator doors open and we step in. "But she wouldn't be the kind of girl you'd change for."

# 40

AMELIA

Ever since seeing his brother, Nick has been doing much better. The moment he came back in the house that night, he told me everything. I didn't ask but I think he felt like he couldn't keep it to himself.

Apparently, they went on a drive, a long drive. Where his brother and he just talked about what they're both going through. Nick told me that he felt like, for the first time in a long time, his brother and he were on the same page. Like they understood each other. It was at that moment he realized they had more in common than they thought.

After the drive, they went to their dad's house. There, they were joined by Nick's sister, Kaitlyn. I haven't met her yet either but I've heard lots about her. Nick says she's dying to meet the woman who made a womanizer a one-woman man, but he's holding off because he's apparently afraid she'll scare me off. My sister can't wait to meet her.

Nick's dad ordered pizza and they all spent time together as a family. Nick needed that. I could tell as he animatedly told me everything that happened later that night. He needed his family just like I needed mine and I was glad they were there for him.

"Get ready, we're going out," Nick says, coming into my room.

I stare at him. "Um, you need to revisit that statement," I respond.

He smiles at me. "Sorry, I forgot who I was talking to for a second," he jokes.

"You sure did," I respond, laughing.

He closes the door behind him and walks the rest of the way in. I've been seated at my desk getting some work done. I've got my last exam this coming week, the one I expect to be the hardest. Still, if law school is the goal, which it is, I need to kick its butts.

"I'd like to take you out," he tells me, then kisses my forehead.

I revel in the feeling. "Take me out where?" I ask.

"Let's do this the right way," he says.

"What do you mean let's do this the right way?" I ask.

"It means I want us to start over," he responds.

I close my laptop then turn my chair fully around so I'm facing him. "Can you be clear?!" I beg.

"My name is Nick Hunter. I'm a football player. I used to be a womanizer but that's not me anymore," he starts, and I laugh at his foolishness. "I think you're beautiful and I have a feeling you're smart too," he adds.

I roll my eyes at him.

"If you'll have me, I'd love to take you out on a date. To a restaurant, where we will be publicly seen by hopefully as many people as possible."

I can't help but smile. We haven't really been out since everything happened. "You're asking me on a date?!"

He nods. "And if the date goes well, which I have a feeling it will, I'd like to take you out on another date and then another."

"Okay," I tell him, taking in his appearance. He's wearing black jeans and a button up. "Seems like you expected me to say yes," I tell him, pointing at his outfit. His boyish smile has returned and I love it. I love him. Even if at first I didn't want to, I couldn't stop myself.

"I mean, I really hoped you would. And now that you've agreed, you should know I haven't had an official girlfriend since elementary school. But that I have a feeling before the date even begins that I'll be asking you to be my first real girlfriend and hopefully my last," he says, taking my hand. I get up from my chair and he pulls me toward him.

"Before the date begins?! You work fast," I tell him as my breath quickens.

He places a kiss on my lips. "Only when I've already had a taste and know what I'm in for."

"I'll let you take me on that very public date, but we'll see how I feel about you at the end of the night before I agree to an official relationship status," I tell him.

"Technically, my family already knows you're my girlfriend," he says then laughs. I love the sound of it. The sound of joy returning.

"Who said I was your girlfriend?" I ask.

He looks at me deviously. "Remember that time I called you my girlfriend in front of my brother then kissed you in front of your sister?" he asks.

I nod.

"You didn't seem to dislike the idea, then," he says, then kisses me again.

He never really asked but he never needed to. "I guess I'm going on a date with my boyfriend, then," I tell him. He hugs me tightly, so much so my feet leave the floor.

Then he kisses me again and again.

———

"This isn't a restaurant," I tell him as we pull up to Eclipse, a bar near school I've never ventured to but have heard a lot about.

He parks in the lot and ignores my statement.

"Nick," I start.

He turns off the car then looks at me. "You trust me, right?" he asks.

"Sometimes," I tell him jokingly.

He exits the car. I take off my seatbelt and, before I have a chance to open the door, he's opening it for me.

"My lady," he says, then bows.

I get out of the car and shake my head. "You're something else."

"We're resetting," he says, taking my hand in his.

I look up at him. "Does that mean you'll be opening doors for me all the time now?" I ask.

He shakes his head. "Don't push it, we haven't even gotten past the first date," he says then we both laugh.

Thinking back, I don't think I've ever laughed so much with another person before. It's like I've had a very serious life and then Nick came into it and brought some of the happiness it was missing.

If I said that to him he'd tell me I'm calling him a clown and that he's brought more than jokes into my life. Then he'd wink at me so I knew exactly what he was referring to. I laugh out loud at the thought.

"What?" he asks.

"Just thinking," I tell him.

"What about?" he asks, just as we round the corner and reach the front door of Eclipse.

We stop in front of it. "At this very second I'm wondering why I got all dressed up to come to this bar," I tell him. "Or why you told me we were going to a restaurant," I add.

"Okay fine, so I lied about starting over," he says to me.

I shake my head. "Lying on the first date is not a good start," I joke.

"I can't start over with you," he says, holding both of my hands and bringing them up to his chest.

"Why not?" I ask.

He places his arm on the small of my back and pulls me toward him. "Because everything we've been through has brought us here. Everything we've lived through together was necessary," he says, his outlook surprising me. "I don't want to start over with you, I want to keep moving forward with you," he adds. I stand there speechless, feeling like I could stay like this with him forever.

I close my eyes and take his words in. "I want to move forward with you too," I tell him.

"See, I told you before the date started I could get you to agree to be my girlfriend and to future dates," he says, then laughs.

I shake my head at this man. "So, I guess we're going in for shots," I tell him, pointing at the door we've been standing in front of. I'm surprised someone hasn't come outside and hit us with it.

"About that," he starts. He takes a step back and I see the telltale sign of his nervousness as his hand moves to the back of his head. "You didn't tell me today was your birthday," he says, his hand coming to the door's handle.

He opens the doors to Eclipse and the voices inside yell "Surprise!"

I look inside to find familiar and unfamiliar faces looking back at me. "I hope you don't mind, your sister and I decided you guys needed a party to celebrate another year of life. She didn't mind that she wouldn't be surprised because she wanted to plan it anyway. I thought you deserved a surprise."

Looking from the group of people to him, I find myself both extremely grateful and a little nervous. "There're a lot of people in there," I tell him.

"Yeaaah," he says nervously. "I may have invited my dad, sister, and a few of the guys on the team," he finishes.

I'm sorry, what? "You're saying I'm going to meet your family right now?" I ask, suddenly overcome with panic.

"I had to meet your dad. I had already met your mom but both of them together was more intimidating," he says.

"Wait, my parents are here?" I look in the room and find my parents smiling in my direction in a corner of the room.

Nick waves at them. "Yup, they're with my dad!" he tells me.

That's scary.

"Are you guys going to come in fully or just stand out there? We have two birthdays to celebrate right now," My sister says, inter-rupting us.

Nick takes my hand and whispers in my ear. "I'd kiss you right now but your parents are watching and they make me nervous."

I catch him off guard, getting on my tippy toes and kissing him right in front of everyone. "Thank you," I tell him.

"I'd do anything for you."

# 41

## AMELIA

I didn't even notice when Thanksgiving passed. No one said anything. No one mentioned it. I guess we weren't really feeling grateful for anything at that point in our lives.

It was a little under a month ago, but it was dark. Too dark. And the loss of our baby was the only thing we could focus on.

In deciding to take steps forward, Nick thought that Christmas Eve was the perfect time for our families to meet without the noise and chaos of the birthday party. My parents went back home because they still had to work but promised to make it back for this dinner.

They showed up two days ago, a day after I submitted my final exam. They're in Elia's room, which means she's in mine, which also meant that Nick went home yesterday. He wasn't too happy about being kicked out of my room, but he's too scared of my dad to try and argue. He also had to help his dad get everything ready.

I think it's funny that he's trying to make sure everything is perfect. I know he just wants to make a good impression on my parents, he wants them to like him. Jokes on him though, to my surprise, my parents love him. They think he's funny and responsible. If anyone had described Nick as responsible to me a few months ago, I would've laughed in their faces. But people do change. Mature. Grow.

"So, when are we supposed to get to his house?" My sister asks, flat ironing her hair in front of the mirror.

I look at my outfit a third time wondering if this is what I should be wearing. I'm wearing dress pants with a nice top. My hair is thrown back in a properly styled ponytailed, courtesy of Elia. "In like an hour but it takes like 30 minutes to get there, so hurry up and finish already," I tell her.

Elia's wearing a cute red dress that's the sort of thing I imagined she would wear. It fits her well and highlights just how different our styles are. "You better tell Mom that, I bet you she'll take way longer than I will," my sister reminds me that if she's bad, Mom's worse when it comes to getting ready.

Maybe I should wear a dress too? I mean, will Nick's father care? Will his sister? Will his brother? I don't even know if his brother is going to be there but I assume his sister will. I got to meet her briefly during the birthday party, but Nick played interference, making sure she never got me alone for too long. I laughed when he told me he was saving me from being interrogated by her. At the time, I really appreciated it.

I look down at my clothes again nervously. I guess Nick isn't the only one trying to win parents over. "Should I change?" I ask my sister.

"You look great. Like a smart, beautiful, future lawyer," my sister says, and I smile at her.

I take a deep breath. "Thank you," I tell her. "Now hurry up!"

"Go rush Mom!" she says in response.

I walk out of my room and knock at my sister's door. "Come in," I hear my mother say. I step into the room to find her wearing dress pants with a beautiful top of her own. She looks absolutely stunning.

I look down at my clothes then at hers. "We're almost matching," I tell her.

"You got your style from me," she responds. "Sometimes I think I'm your twin and not Elia," she adds, and I laugh. I could see that.

Turning to Dad, I find him struggling to tie his tie. "Need help, Dad?" I ask, already walking toward him.

He looks down at what he's doing then at me. "Please, your mom's been getting herself ready and I thought I could do it for myself."

"You're lost without her, not sure how you stayed alive before you met her," I joke, undoing his tie and starting over.

"Not sure how I lived before I met any of you," he responds lovingly.

I finish a few seconds later and my dad looks at me surprised. "How is it that you can do this so quickly and I can't do it at all?" he asks.

"Talent," my mother and I say at the exact same time, which makes us all laugh.

"You look wonderful," Dad says.

"Thank you," I respond, straightening out my shirt.

He takes my hand, stopping me from continuing to mess with my shirt. "Are you nervous?" he asks.

I nod. "It's a sit-down dinner at his house with his family and mine and who knows who else. How could I not be nervous?" I tell him. The party was at least drowned out by noise and other people. This seems more formal.

"I'm nervous too," Dad responds with an unsure smile of his own.

I'm surprised. "Why are you nervous?" I ask.

"I just met your boyfriend and his family at your birthday and now we're going to have Christmas Eve dinner with them," he starts, and I smile like a lovesick idiot when he says boyfriend. "I feel like next time I see him, it'll be your wedding," he jokes.

I open my eyes wide and hold back laughter. "Let's not push it," I tell him. If only he knew how many times a week Nick asks me to marry him.

"Oh, trust me, I'm not trying to push it. Not even a little. I'd actually like for it all to slow down," he replies.

My mother walks up to us. "Stop it, you two. It'll be fine."

I know it'll be fine but it doesn't make it any less nerve-wrecking.


## NICK

I FEEL LIKE IT'S CHRISTMAS DAY ALREADY AND I'M A FIVE-YEAR-OLD eager to see what gifts will be waiting for me under the tree. Except this time, I'm twenty-one years old and just eager to see my girlfriend and my friend.

When Dad mentioned hosting a Christmas Eve dinner, I jumped at the opportunity. I wanted to have all the people I cared about in one room. It'd be a lot easier to make fun of them if I had them all here at once.

The one sucky thing is that I can't be extra wild because parents are coming. I have to be on my best behavior and try to not make a fool of myself. I'll have to try real hard because being a clown is really my number one job.

This is serious though.

I look at the watch and put the finishing touch on my Christmas outfit. I decided to wear slacks and a button up. No tie or jacket, though, I'm not that desperate.

Coming down the stairs, I run into my dad, who's wearing an ugly Christmas sweater. "Really, Dad?" I tell him, judging the crap out of his clothing choice.

"What? Is this not good enough?" he responds.

I shake my head. "No, sir. Please go find a shirt."

"Yes, sir," he says, saluting me and then going back upstairs.

I love the guy. Seriously. He's a lot happier now that he's not with Mom. I bet you he'd be even happier with a woman of his own. He's a Hunter after all.

Walking into the kitchen briefly, I see the ten caterers Dad hired for this. It was supposed to be a small Christmas dinner but then I just kept inviting people and it got out of hand. We needed someone else to come here and handle all the hard stuff.

The bell rings and I rush to the door to welcome in our first guest, hoping it's Amelia. When I reach the door, I'm disappointed to see it's just my sister on the other side. "Where are your keys?"

"Merry Christmas to you too, brother," she says, walking past me.

I roll my eyes. "Can you help Dad find a proper shirt?" I ask her.

"Since when do you care about Dad's clothes?" she asks, then realization dawns. "Aww, are you trying to impress your girlfriend's family?"

"Shut up!" I shout back, only to hear her laugh as she walks up the stairs to hopefully help Dad. We may get on each other's nerves but we've got each other's back. It's a twin thing or maybe it's a Hunter thing since Colton has our backs too.

I LOOK AT MY WATCH AND NOTICE THE OFFICIAL START TIME IS IN fifteen minutes. Just as I grab my phone from my back pocket, the bell rings again. Eagerly, I open it. "Hi, Nick!" Mia says then wraps her arms around me. "It's been so long, how are you?" she asks excitedly. She's really nice.

"I'm good! How are you?" I tell her. My brother shows up behind her a few seconds later.

"She's mine," he responds and I laugh.

"I know, brother. I know," I tell him. "I've got my own," I add.

Mia smiles. "You sure do and I cannot wait to meet her! Is she here already?" she asks.

I shake my head. "Not yet."

"Okay, well, I'll be on the lookout," she says and I move out the way so they can enter.

I walk over to the living room with them. "Could you keep Kaitlyn away from her?" I ask.

Mia shrugs. "I'll try, but you know your sister."

"What about his sister?" Kaitlyn chooses that time to pop into the living room. They both squeal when they see each other and Colton and I take that as our opportunity to head to the kitchen and grab a beer.

MY DAD WALKS INTO THE KITCHEN A FEW MINUTES LATER AND GIVES Colton a bear hug. Then, he tells the caterers that they're good to go. I figured he'd get them to prepare the meals but not stay here to serve them. It is Christmas Eve after all and I bet they have places to be.

"Mr. Hunter, how are you?" I hear Zack say from behind us. The door must've stayed open because I didn't hear the bell. That or he knocked on the door instead of pressing the button and the girls let him in.

My dad gives him a hug before I can get to him. "You know you have to call me William, Will even," he tells him.

Zack nods. "I'll take William," he says with a smile. "Little Nicky, come here!" he tells me, then traps me in his own bear hug.

"Watch the hair!" I tell him.

"You've gone soft," he jokes

I punch him lightly in the stomach. "So have you it seems!" I reply.

"Are your parents here, Zack?" my dad asks. I bet he's ready for some adults.

Zack nods. "They're in the living room."

"I'll go find them," my dad says.

In true Zack fashion, he walks over to Colton and hugs him as well. My brother tolerates it and eventually pushes him off when Zack takes too long. Zack and I laugh because we know how to press Colton's buttons. "Where's Emma?" I ask.

"With the girls," he responds.

THE THREE OF US WALK OVER TO THE LIVING ROOM, WITH BEERS IN hand, and join the rest of the arrivals. We exchange greetings and jokes.

The doorbell goes off again and I walk toward it, hoping it's Amelia so I can be off door duty. I want to be the first person she sees when she gets here. I know she's going to be nervous, especially walking into a house full of football players, their girlfriends, and their parents.

Sadly, it's not Amelia at the door. But I guess Chase isn't so bad. I open it and he steps right in. "Is your girlfriend finally here?" my sister says, walking out of the living room and toward the front door. She stops in her tracks when she sees Chase.

I really want to say, 'no, but your boyfriend is' so badly. "No, but Chase is," I say instead. I'm not going to meddle, despite how much I want to. Colton told me it wasn't my place, and for once I'm going to listen.

"I didn't know you were coming," she says, and I take a step back so I'm not in the line of fire. I'll stay for the drama though.

Chase looks at me then her. "I was invited," he responds.

"Did you bring your girlfriend?" she asks, and man, my sister sounds jealous.

Chase closes the door behind him. I guess that answers that. "I'll let you two be," I tell them and then get the heck out of here and join the others in the living room.

I'M TALKING TO THE GUYS AND WAITING FOR CHASE AND KAITLYN TO come back in the room. "Are Jesse and Zoe coming?" my dad asks.

I shake my head.

"They're doing a dinner at Zoe's parents. Both of their families will be there instead," Mia replies.

"How's he doing?" Dad asks, still standing in the other corner of the room with Zack's parents and Emma's mom.

We barely see him anymore. "It's been a busy year for him. Med school applications plus classes has been a lot to handle," Emma responds. I think everyone stops to look at her when she speaks. I guess we're still shocked she's not this super shy girl.

Makes sense that Emma would know about their plans, Zoe was

her roommate after all, though now she lives with Jesse. Emma moved in with my sister to Mia's old place.

Kaitlyn and Chase walk in and our attention turns to them. Chase waves hello and heads straight to where the guys are seated. Kaitlyn joins the girls on the other couch.

The bell rings again and I get up like the couch is on fire.

There's only one person missing from this dinner and that's the one I care about the most.

# 42

## AMELIA

The GPS tells Dad that our destination is on our right. "Wait, that's his house?" My sister says, surprised, and I'm right there with her. "That's not a house. That's a mansion," she adds.

The home is huge, I'll give her that. It makes ours look like a shoebox. "Wow," I say from the backseat as my dad parks the car on the curb.

"Of course you'd find a rich boyfriend," my sister jokes. I pin her with a look. "I'm kidding, I'm kidding," she responds.

"Hm, you better be." I tell her. "I don't care about his money," I add, making it clear.

Mom looks back at me. "He clearly comes from wealth," she says. There's no judgment in her voice.

I look down at what I'm wearing, hating that I didn't change it before. Then, I shake that thought out of my head. I don't have to be whatever I think someone else wants me to. I just have to be me. If that's not good enough for them, that's fine.

I close my eyes and take a deep breath. I've already met Nick's dad, brother, and sister. His dad was kind. His brother intimidating. And his twin sister, well, she's very much like mine.

"Are we ready?" Dad says, turning off the car.

"It's now or never," I respond, taking off my seatbelt and getting out.

My family follows behind me as I make my way to the front door. I feel my palms start to get sweaty and I wipe them on my pants. *Relax, Amelia.* I tell myself as I bring my hand to the bell and ring it.

The door opens and I instantly smile when I see Nick's face. "Hi!" Nick says. He goes for a kiss but then places it on my cheek when he sees my parents standing behind me.

Elia giggles.

"Mr. and Mrs. King, welcome!" Nick says, leading the way into the house.

"You're not going to welcome me?" Elia protests.

Nick throws his arm around her. "Hey there, little sis."

We all follow Nick inside. The house is more gorgeous on the inside than I expected. I'm taking it all in when I hear the voices of people chatting. "How many people are here?" I ask him when he comes to stand next to me.

He bites his lip. "Only a few," he says, and I don't believe a word he says. "You look beautiful, by the way," he whispers in my ear.

"You don't look so bad yourself," I tell him.

"Everyone's in the living room chatting. Let's head there so I can introduce y'all," Nick says, and I look back at my mom, seeking encouragement.

"You've got this, sweetie," she mouths.

We reach the living room and there is the confirmation that when Nick said a few, he meant more than a dozen. There's pockets of people all over the room. One corner has a couple of tall, muscular guys who I assume are football players. Among them is Colton

Hunter. He looks just as serious as he did the day he showed up at our apartment.

On the other corner of the room, I recognize Nick's sister talking animatedly to two other girls. And finally, I spot Nick's dad talking to a bunch of adults.

"Hey guys," Nick says, and the room is instantly quiet as all eyes turn to us. He places his hand around me and pulls me to him. "This is my girlfriend Amelia, her twin sister Elia, and her parents!" he says, by way of introduction.

One of the guys, a red head, starts clapping. "About time!" he shouts.

"Shut up," Nick tells him.

His dad comes over and greets us. "Mr. and Mrs. King, let me introduce you to some of the other parents. We're trying to keep our distance from these youngins," he jokes.

My sister looks at me as she tries to stop herself from laughing at William calling us youngins. Mom and Dad follow behind him and join the rest of the adults at the other side of the room.

"Let me take your coats. I forgot to ask your parents too, so I'll do that and put them away for now," Nick says. Elia and I remove our coats and hand them to him. Then we watch him walk toward our parents and take theirs.

"Hi, I'm Mia," a sweet brunette says, coming out of nowhere. "It's so nice to finally meet you. Colton's told me a bit about you," she says. The other girls join us.

Oh.

"Sorry, I didn't mean that in a bad way at all. I'm his girlfriend," she says.

Kaitlyn clears her throat. "Fiancée," she clarifies, pointing at the massive ring on her finger.

Mia looks down at her hand. "Sorry, I forget sometimes."

"Don't let him hear that," Kaitlyn says, laughing.

Mia looks back at Colton and, almost as though he feels it, he looks back at her at that exact moment and smiles. I guess he does smile after all. Nick was right, Mia definitely changes him.

"I'm Emma," the blonde girl says, adjusting her glasses. "The red headed fool who was clapping earlier is my boyfriend," she says, shaking her head. Interesting pairing. Reminds me of Nick and me if I'm being honest. He's the clown and I'm the serious one.

"I'm Elia, her twin," my sister says, introducing herself.

The girls look back and forth between the two of us. "You guys are twins and you're dating a twin?" Emma says, sounding shocked. I don't know what the odds of that are. "The two of you don't look very much alike," Emma adds.

"Not all twins look like each other," Kaitlyn responds, echoing my sentiments.

"That's very true," Mia adds.

Nick comes back into the room. He sees the girls surrounding me and with his eyes asks me if I'm okay. I nod slightly and that's his cue to go and join the guys.

"Kaitlyn, is the other guy over there your boyfriend?" I ask, curious. So the red headed guy is dating Emma, Colton is with Mia, and Nick is mine. It would make sense that all the boyfriends would be here.

"No," she says, more quickly than I expected.

Emma and Mia laugh. "That's a whole story we'll explain to you next time we hang out," Mia says.

"Nothing to explain!" Kaitlyn argues and I know I've asked the wrong question.

Mia rests her hand on my shoulder. "There's a lot and nothing there," she tells me.

"I mean, if you're not interested, I wouldn't mind," my sister says, surprising us and not reading the room very well. "I'm kidding, I'm kidding," she responds, and all the girls burst out laughing after seeing the look in Kaitlyn's eyes.

"Sorry, didn't mean to pry," I tell her when we all stop laughing.

Kaitlyn shakes it off. "Ignore me! He's already pissed me off today. Pry away, it's what I do anyway," she says then smiles at me, making me feel less tense.

"Who are all the adults?" my sister asks.

"Nick said it was going to be a small gathering, but from the looks of it, it's definitely a dinner party," I tell them, already feeling comfortable around them.

Mia rolls her eyes. "Yeah, no such thing as small when it comes to the Hunters."

"Mia, that's so inappropriate!" Kaitlyn exclaims and Mia's eyes widen and her cheeks redden.

"That's not what I was talking about!" she responds, shaking her head.

We all laugh. "I get what you mean," I tell her, enjoying the moment.

"So, Zack's parents are here, that's those two," she says, pointing. "Then, that's my dad, step mom, and little sister," Mia says, and I notice the little girl for the first time.

Emma picks up where Mia left off. "That's my mom over there. My dad is coming later, which will be all sorts of fun," she finishes sarcastically.

"Why do you say that?" I ask.

"Because he's the head coach at Bragan," she says.

"Oh, so Nick and the guys play for them?" I ask.

Mia shakes her head. "Zack, Colton, and Chase are all in the NFL, so just Nick now. But yeah, they all used to," she tells me. I knew about Colton, but I did not know we were in a room full of professional football players right now. If I knew more about football I'd probably be more excited. At this point, I'm just happy to be happy.

"So wait, you dated a player your dad was coaching?" my sister asks, focusing on what was most important to her.

Emma nods. "Yeah, that was something else," she says with a smile as she readjusts her glasses.

"Badass," Elia responds.

"So, you'll have to tell us more about how you and Nick started dating," Mia says.

"How's that all going?" Emma adds.

"I mean, Nick's always been—" Kaitlyn starts, and Nick chooses that precise time to walk over and interrupt.

"If you don't mind, I want to introduce my girlfriend to the guys," he says, then takes my hand and pulls me away from the group. I leave my sister and the girls behind and head nervously toward the corner of NFL players.

---

EMMA'S DAD JOINED US A FEW MINUTES LATER AND WE ALL TOOK OUR seats in the dining room. The table was beautifully set and the girls and parents took their seats as the guys brought over the first course of the night to the table. Yes, I said first course, apparently, there were multiple meals planned.

I tried not to look too amazed at every little thing but I'm sure it wasn't working.

The guys walk in with plates in hand, and only after each person has a plate do they take their seats. Kaitlyn suggested the girls sit on one side of the table and the guys sit on the others but Colton vetoed that plan really quickly. He was sitting next to Mia whether we wanted him to or not. Then, everything shuffled around and Nick ended up sitting next to me. My sister sat next to Mom. Emma next to her boyfriend. William was at the head of the table with parents on his left and right. My favorite pairing of the night was Chase and Kaitlyn. Somehow, they ended up sitting next to each other. It was fun watching her make faces at him the whole night. Nick was enjoying watching them too. I'm sure he'll tell me more about what's going on later.

Before we start eating, Mr. Hunter, William, as he insisted I call him, raises his glass and we all turn our attention to him. "I just want to thank you all for taking time out of your holiday to enjoy this meal with us," he starts and we all start thanking him for inviting us.

"I want to say a few things and I hope you will indulge me," William continues. "First, I want to tell you it makes me incredibly happy to see our family growing," he says, looking around the table.

I take in the smiling faces and realize this is exactly that. A large family. A family Nick has welcomed me into.

"Aww, Dad!" Nick says dramatically, and his dad shakes his head.

"Mia, I know you were raised celebrating Christmas today so, Feliz Navidad!" he says, raising his glass of wine and toasting.

"Feliz Navidad!" We all say.

Mia looks like she's about to cry and I watch as Colton's hand moves to hers. "Feliz Navidad," Mia responds, raising her own glass.

"This year we have gained a lot," he says, looking around the room. "And we have had some deep losses," he says, his eyes stopping briefly when he reaches Nick and me. I hold back the tears as I think about our baby. It still hurts but sitting here, surrounded by loved ones, and also strangers, I know it'll get better. "May we learn. May we move forward. And may we hold on to each other," he finishes his toast.

"I'd like to make a toast of my own," Emma's dad says.

I watch the way Emma instantly turns her head toward him as she watches him expectantly. "While some of you are in the NFL and probably not paying too much attention to little old college football anymore," he starts, "Our Championship game is next month and Nick and the team could use the support," he says. "Here's to victory. May it be swift," he adds and we all cheer.

"Let's go, LIONS!" Zack says, and Coach just looks at him and shakes his head.

"Let's go, Lions!" Nick and the rest of the guys at the table echo it.

Jumping right along, Nick gets everyone's attention by tapping his glass with a spoon. "I've got one too," he says and everyone groans. "Ouch!" he says, pretending to be hurt.

"Go ahead," Zack says. I've realized tonight that Zack is like Nick's personal cheerleader, always encouraging his crazy.

"First of all, I want to welcome in the King's to our family," he says, and I smile. "And now, can we please eat because the food's getting cold and I'm hungry!" he adds and we all laugh.

THE REST OF THE NIGHT GOES BY SMOOTHLY. THE GUYS AND GIRLS laugh and talk while the parents seem to be in their own bubble. We joke and make fun of one another. We appreciate the time we get to spend together and we get to know each other. We make plans for the future and we exchange contact information.

It's the best Christmas I've ever had and, as the night comes to an end, I find myself just being grateful for all of it.

# 43

## AMELIA

Okay, so people really love football. I mean, I've always known football was a big deal at Bragan, but being in New Jersey waiting for the championship game to be played, I know for a fact that there is a football obsession.

All these people traveled here from different parts of the country to see two teams of colleges students, athletes, play against each other.

I mean, I'm here because my boyfriend is playing his last college game ever and it's really important to him. But most of these people don't even know the players aside from just watching them on TV, and yet they're walking around with Lion costumes on.

"This is crazy," I tell the girls as we walk around and take in the sight.

Kaitlyn nods. "It's like this every time," she tells me. She doesn't look phased by this at all.

"How often do you go to these?" I ask.

She sighs. "Often enough," she responds.

"Thanks for taking us in," I tell the girls as we walk toward the stadium gate. If Emma and Kaitlyn didn't come to the game and reach out to us so we could all come here together, Dimah and I would've been navigating this on our own. That would've been intimidating since neither of us has done this before.

"Me too!" Dimah says, echoing my sentiments. I met her briefly two nights ago. The guys wanted to introduce us so that we could keep each other company during our stay and during the game. She's really sweet. Quiet but kind.

"She took me in once too; don't say thank you too early," Emma adds and we laugh.

"You met Zack because of me!" Kaitlyn argues.

"Not sure if that's a good thing!" Emma responds.

Kaitlyn rolls her eyes as we wait in line to be let into the game, "Shut up, you know you're in love with him."

Emma just smiles. "Fineee," she says, giving in. "I'll give you that."

"So, Dimah, Lincoln seems to be a really good guy," I tell her. I've noticed that out of all the girls in the group, she's the most reserved. Yet she's also the one I feel like if I talked to, I would have the most things in common with.

Dimah smiles. "He is," she tells me.

"Nick raves about him all the time," I tell her.

We move up in the line. "Nick seems pretty cool too," she tells me.

"He'd like to think so," I joke and we all laugh.

We make it through the line and walk over to our seats. "I'll go grab some snacks," Kaitlyn says when we take our seats.

"I'll come with!" Emma tells her.

"Let me get you some cash," I start, getting up to grab my money from my back pocket and I watch Dimah do the same.

"You ladies are good. It's your first time here, so it's my treat," Kaitlyn says in a voice that tells me she will take no budge on this.

"Thank you," Dimah and I both say at the same time, knowing better than to argue with Kaitlyn.

"Any preferences?" Emma asks.

I shake my head. "I'll take an orange soda and some nachos. Hope that's okay." It feels weird to order things when I'm not paying. "I can come with if you guys want?" I offer.

"You girls are good to stay! We'll be back right away, don't let anyone take our seats," Kaitlyn says, and I wonder if people do that. "What about you, Dimah?" Kaitlyn adds.

"I'll also take some nachos but with a Coke, please!" She responds.

As the girls leave, we're joined by Nick's dad, Colton, and Mia. "Hi, girls!" she says when she spots us. "I guess we're all on the same row," she tells me.

"Oh, that was intentional," William says. "Nick wanted to make sure he knew where we'd all be cheering for him," he adds.

"Doesn't surprise me one bit," I tell him, giving him a hug. Colton waves at me and Mia rolls her eyes.

A few seconds later, Kaitlyn and Emma return. They say hi to everyone then take their seats next to us, with Kaitlyn taking the seat closest to me.

"That was faster than I thought it would be!" I tell them.

She hands me the nachos and drink. "And I even got some shopping done!" she adds then opens a plastic bag and pulls out two jerseys.

I look at her and Emma and notice that they're already wearing Bragan shirts.

"Here you go," Kaitlyn says, handing a jersey to me and one to Dimah. Dimah unfolds hers and smiles when she sees Lincoln's name on the back.

"You didn't have to, thank you!" Dimah says, still smiling. She throws it over her shirt and that's when I unfold mine already knowing what to expect. That was really kind of Kaitlyn and likely very costly. I know better than to argue with her though, I'll just have to think of something nice to do in return.

Nick's last name is the first thing I see when I look at the jersey.

"Seriously, you didn't have to!" I tell her, putting the jersey on over my blue shirt.

"No need! I'm sure the guys will be really happy when they see the two of you with their jerseys on. If they see you from the field, who knows, you may motivate them," she tells us.

"I'm sure they'll appreciate it!" I tell her.

She nods. "I'm sure Nick will for sure. I don't know Lincoln, but I know when my brother sees you with his jersey on, you may want to hide," she jokes.

"I can vouch for that!" Mia says, then looks at Colton.

"I'm surprised you're not wearing a jersey right now!" Kaitlyn tells Mia.

"We're trying to go for anonymity," she explains. Maybe that's why this is the first time I see Colton wearing a hat. He's got a bit of a five-o-clock shadow too. I wonder if that's part of his disguise. "Can't do that if we're both wearing Hunter jerseys," she finishes.

WE SIT THERE AND TALK FOR A LONG TIME. THE SEATS FILL UP SLOWLY until it seems there's not a single seat available in the stadium. Our attention goes straight onto the field as the guys come out and the game begins. I sit at the edge of my seat. I may not understand football but that doesn't mean I don't understand the importance of this for Nick. It's his last college game and hopefully the one that seals his future for him. From here to the NFL, that's what he wants, and so that's what I want.

I don't think I've ever said this before but when the crowd chants, "Let's go Lions!" I join them.

## NICK

I SIT IN THE VISITOR LOCKER AND REALIZATION HITS ME: THIS IS THE final game of my college career. A game where I have to play my best to make up for that one game I lost terribly, where I wasn't necessarily the best player on the field. I need to have one of those games that make my name known to those who still don't know me.

Now, more than ever, I need to make waves. I need to be seen. I've applied for the draft and need to make sure I put myself in a good position to be drafted. I need to make game winning plays tonight. But above all, I need to win.

"Are we ready?!" I scream in the guys' ears as they sit in front of the lockers. "LETS WIN THIS!" I shout again. Winning is my singular goal today.

"Let's do it!" they shout back.

"Hey, Hunter," I hear Lincoln yell from behind me. "We've got this," he says with a smile on his face. I finally got to meet his girl-friend. He asked if it would be okay for her to hang out with Amelia and my family this weekend. I said absolutely and made sure she had the seat next to Amelia. With how discrete Lincoln is, if he were asking me that it's because he wanted to make sure she wasn't alone. My job is to make sure my quarterback has nothing but winning on his mind.

"Are you ready to throw some dimes my way?" I ask him.

He nods. "You're in a good mood," he tells me.

"You'll see it out on the field today," I reply cockily. Because that's the kind of mood I'm in, a showing off one.

Lincoln shakes his head. "Good!"

"You're going to miss my talent on this team," I tell him.

Truth is, despite how much I wanted to rush the process, I'm glad Dad forced me to stay the extra year. I mean, for one, it gave me Amelia. It also gave me the chance to be my own person, without living in my brother's shadow. This will be the first championship without my brother playing on the same team.

"I sure am," he responds.

"Are you ready for this?" I ask him. This is the biggest stage he's ever played on. I've been here before. I've won this before.

He nods. "I'm done losing." I know he had a winning record at least for his last two years of high school, so when he says he's done losing, I know he means in more than just football. I don't question him though; a winning mentality is what we need right now.

JUST AS WE'RE ALL DONE GETTING READY, COACH WILSON WALKS IN. "Huddle up," he announces. My mind wanders to Christmas Eve dinner where I actually got to see him outside of football for the first time ever. I mean, I guess he wasn't really out of football since he spent most of the time talking about the upcoming game, but still he seemed more relaxed. The guy loves football more than the rest of us do, which is unbelievable. I'm going to miss getting on his nerves, though I'm sure if things between Zack and Emma go well, I'll be seeing more of him in the future.

My teammates are silent as we surround Coach and wait for him to give us marching orders. He looks around the room at each of us, the tension rising as we all wait eagerly. "Tonight isn't just another game," he starts. "Tonight is the game we've been working toward since the last time we found ourselves on this national stage. It's up to us to win. Make every play count. Make every second count. WHO ARE WE?" he shouts.

"LIONS!" we all answer in unison.

Coach signals to me and I know that's my cue to say something. I'm the captain after all and this is my last game. "How are we feeling right now?!" I ask, and the guys all scream in response. "We're ready for this. We've got this. We've come this far and we won't leave without that trophy!" I tell them. I'm not about to give a sappy speech about this being my last game and whatnot. We don't have time for those emotions. We need to stay focused.

---

"HE MISSES A WIDE OPEN HUNTER," THE ANNOUNCER SAYS. I DON'T usually listen to them announce the plays, but as I walk back over to the bench, I can't help but notice.

I watch Lincoln as he reaches the bench, his posture defeated.

The offensive coordinator walks over to him and tells him a few things. Lincoln nods, taking it all in. I turn around and look at the sea of people. Then, I look at the scoreboard. It's the second quarter and we've got 3 points on the board from a field goal kicked in the first four minutes of the first quarter by Rodriguez. I look at the opponent's score: 21.

Our kicking team kicks the ball and I watch from the sideline as the opposing team moves the chains. The drive takes six minutes off the clock and is sealed by yet another touchdown. 28 to 3. That's the new score.

With a minute left in the second quarter, we finally take the field. Lincoln calls the play and the moment the ball is snapped, I run. I run left and right as I try to dodge the two defenders guarding me. I turn to watch as Lincoln throws yet another incomplete pass to one of our wide receivers.

We get back in the huddle. Another play is called. The ball is snapped and I focus on tackling my man as our running back tries to push the ball enough yards to get us our only first down of the game. He's taken down before he gets there.

So, we huddle all over again and I try to block out the noise coming from the crowd. This is our biggest stage and we're failing.

Another snap. Another incomplete pass. Another whistle. Then we're leaving the field with no time on the clock. Our fans no longer cheering for us but wondering why our team is falling apart. Our teammates hang their heads on the way back to the locker room.

When we get inside, Coach goes off. He tells us we need to do better, using words that are less kind. I watch as Lincoln shakes his head in disappointment and I know that he's feeling it right now, the pressure to perform. Pressure can do one of two things, it can help you or it can destroy you.

. . .

A FEW MINUTES LATER, HALFTIME IS OVER AND WE TAKE THE FIELD again. I walk over to Lincoln and throw my arm over his shoulder.

"Look," I tell him. Then, I point at the row where I noticed our family was sitting earlier. Luckily, we got front row seats for them, so they're not hard to spot in this giant field. "You have to remember who we're playing for," I tell him.

I can tell the moment he sees his girlfriend wearing his jersey. At the same time, I realize mine is doing the same. It's the first time I've allowed myself to look in their direction because I've been ashamed of the terrible way we've been playing to make eye contact. "I don't know what's happening," he tells me.

"It's a big stage. It's okay to be nervous. But let's leave all that in the first half. This is the second half now. Time to show everyone why you're our quarterback. Remember though, we're not playing for the fans or the crowds. We're playing for them," I tell him, pointing at the girls.

Though at first I was playing to impress the world, at this very moment I realized that this game is not about them. "I'm playing for Amelia and the child we lost. Who are you playing for?" I ask.

"I'm playing for Dimah and my little brother, Ethan," he says and I feel the certainty in his words when they leave his mouth.

"Alright, so let's go out there and show them."


LINCOLN TAKES A FINAL KNEE AS THE CLOCK RUNS DOWN. THE MOMENT it does, we all jump up and down and hug each other. We scream, some of the guys cry, and we cheer. Not only did we make a comeback the second half, but we won. "I can't believe we won!" One of the guys shouts.

"I can," Lincoln responds. "Thank you," he tells me.

I hug him. "I should be the one thanking you. I feel like I've set a record for most catches in a game now!" I tell him.

"You got some touchdowns in too," he tells me. I don't need the reminder. Our defense held our opponents to one field goal during the second half, bringing their score to 31. We made up the difference by scoring a field goal plus four touchdowns of our own. I scored three of them. Lincoln ran it for one.

"We were unstoppable," I tell him.

He smiles. "That's because the people we play for make us invincible," he responds. Two years ago, I would've barfed at that statement. But today, I know there's nothing more truthful than that.

Amelia makes me feel like I can do anything, and today, all I wanted to do was make her and Nick Jr. proud.

# EPILOGUE

## PART I

## AMELIA

I t's draft day. And by that, I mean the weekend where Nick's future is decided. Nick and I lie in bed early in the morning enjoying the last bit of alone time we're going to have together today. I know it's going to be a stressful day for him, especially if his name isn't called the first round, which I'm certain it will. I don't know how it works but I know he's really good at football, at least that's what the announcers kept saying.

I can't believe we're already in April. After the holidays and the National Championship, it felt like everything sped up. Like time flew by. Honestly, it was more low-key and just what we needed to re-center ourselves. To continue pushing forward. We miss our baby every day, but Mom was right, slowly you learn to live with it. You learn to keep living.

I turn to the side and rest my hand on Nick's chest, feeling his heart beat. "I've always been curious about something," I tell him. He runs his fingers through my hair.

"What?" he asks, turning sideways so he's facing me. I enjoy the feeling of being with him like this. Just the two of us.

I think about how to phrase the question but decide to just go for it. "Why were you on a dating site?" I ask.

"That's random."

"Seriously though. I mean, Nick Hunter on a dating site didn't make much sense considering your reputation. You could've had any girl you wanted," I tell him, hating how true the statement is.

He lowers his head and captures my lips with his. The kiss becomes more intense and our hands move about, exploring every edge and curve of each other's body. I pull back and he moves toward me again. "Wait! You gotta answer," I tell him and he pouts before dropping back on the bed.

"Some of the football players were talking about this hookup site a few days before the draft last year. I was bored and figured why not? I'm not going to lie; I could've slept with any girl I wanted whenever I wanted. But the app seemed like a way to find different girls."

"Different girls," I say, repeating his words. Although it stings a little that he could have any girl he wants, we both know how this started. We both know how the other feels. He doesn't have to hide his past because I know it well, most people do. "Why?" I ask.

"I had a rule," he says, leaving me wondering.

"Nick had rules?! What?" I say, mocking him. "What rule was this?" I ask.

"I didn't sleep with the same girl more than once. So, I figured the app would let me meet new people."

"Interesting," I say, thinking about his answer. "Makes sense," I add.

"I could've had any girl I wanted," he pauses. "I just didn't realize that the app would lead me to the one I needed," he adds.

I pin him with a questionable look as goosebumps spread through me. "I don't know about all that!"

"Matching with me was the best thing you've ever done!" He argues jokingly.

It honestly was the best thing that could've happened. Yes, I could have avoided pain if I hadn't met him, but I also wouldn't know love, not in the way I do now. "I didn't match with you, you have Elia to thank for that," I remind him because this is what we do. We make fun of each other. We bicker. Banter. It's the way it works, the way this works.

"I'll do that next time I see her. You should thank her too. I mean, you ended up with me in the end," he says, pulling me on top of him.

"Too early to tell," I joke. Then he places his hand on my face and kisses me.

## NICK

I'VE NEVER BEEN MORE NERVOUS IN MY LIFE. I GUESS MEETING AMELIA'S parents was a close second. But still. Today is terrifying.

"Are you okay?" she asks from the kitchen of the Football House. Yes, the Football House is where we're watching the draft because that's what we did last year and the results were pretty good. I can only hope for something similar today.

I grab a beer from the fridge. "I'll be fine," I tell her.

"You deserve this," she says, walking over and planting a kiss on my lips.

"Definitely feel better now," I tell her after she backs away. "Can we do that again?" I ask, half-jokingly.

She shakes her head. "People will be here soon."

"Right," I tell her. On cue, I hear the front door open and Colton, Zack, and Chase walk in. It's Friday, so as long as I get picked today, they're good to be here. They all had practice earlier today and have a walk-through tomorrow, so the fact that they made it here tonight means a lot to me. I won't tell them that though.

Right behind them are Emma, Kaitlyn, and Mia. "Welcome to the Football House!" I tell them.

"This is cleaner than I expected," Zack jokes.

"For real," Colton adds.

I shrug. "Let's just say with new leadership, the team learned a bit about getting everything in order," I say smugly.

"Damn, he just said you were a bad leader," Zack turns to Colton and says.

"Where's Amelia?" Mia asks. I point to the kitchen and all the girls walk in that direction. I guess they don't have time to deal with us poking fun at each other.

"Are you ready?" My brother asks.

"I'm just hoping it goes well," I tell them.

"I have no doubt," Zack says.

The door opens again and I turn my attention to see my quarterback walk in through the door with his girlfriend. "Zack this is Lincoln, Colton's replacement, and his girlfriend Dimah." I announce. Colton met Lincoln and Dimah at the championship game. Zack couldn't make it because he had an away game that Sunday but he watched it on TV.

"That was a gem of a game," Zack says, and he doesn't have to say which game he's referring to. Obviously, it's the championship game where Lincoln completed all of his passes during the second half. The comeback made the first half forgettable.

He lowers his head, "Thank you."

"I'm sure Nick gave you crap about not living in the football house, but I don't blame you one bit," Zack says, bringing that up out of nowhere.

I look at Lincoln, who smiles. "He did but he came to terms with it."

"I bet I can tell you exactly when that happened," Zack jokes then points at the kitchen.

Of course Zack would say that. I knew as soon as I settled down with a girl, the guys wouldn't let me hear the end of it. "It was before that... but that made it better," I respond.

"Yeah, he barely spends time here anymore," Lincoln says, referring to the Football House.

"How would you know?" I ask.

"The guys complain to me about it all the time," he replies.

I shake my head. "Talking behind my back. Tsk Tsk."

"Like you don't talk about us behind ours," Lincoln fires back.

"Dimah, is that you?" Amelia says. "Come over to the kitchen," she adds. Dimah looks relieved to be able to join Amelia and the girls and leave us to our pissing contest.

The door opens again and Elia saunters right in. "Girls?" she asks, looking at the group of guys gathered in the living room and wanting nothing to do with it.

"Kitchen," I tell her, pointing in that direction.

"Great!" she says, following my finger and disappearing into the kitchen.

We all take a seat. "I can't believe you're a twin dating a twin," Zack says. "I bet you guys will have twins," he adds. "Oh crap, I'm sorry," he says, realizing what he just said.. These guys all know what happened. I told Zack and Lincoln. I'm sure Colton told Chase since they're still inseparable.

I smile. "No worries, man. I'm excited for the day when we have twins," I tell him.

The door opens again and I turn my attention to it. "Oh Dad, I didn't know if you were going to make it!" I tell him.

He walks over to us and plops down on the sofa next to Colton. "I remember being a Bragan man myself," Dad says looking around the room.

"Back in your younger and better years," I tell him. "You're old now."

"Shut up," my dad says.

"Thanks for coming," I reply.

"I wouldn't miss this for the world," he responds.

The door opens another time, interrupting our chatter. "You guys have no idea who I ran into outside," Jesse says just as he walks in through the door.

"Man, it's been a while. I was starting to think you didn't go here anymore," I joke.

He laughs. "Yeah, it's been tough but I couldn't miss this and apparently, neither could he," he announces and then none other than Blake walks in through the door.

"Holy crap, now it's a party!" I announce. "I haven't seen you in forever!" I tell him, running over to him and giving him a hug.

Zoe and Kiya walk in behind them. "We couldn't miss this," Kiya says.

"Is that Kiya?" I hear Mia before I see her. "Oh my goodness!! Kiya! Zoe," she exclaims then runs across the room to hug her friends. I thought the Christmas Eve dinner was a big reunion but this one takes the cake.

The girls all head to the kitchen and I'm tempted to make a joke out of it but think better of it. Today's not the day. Instead, I catch up with the guys and try to shake off the nerves.

# EPILOGUE

## PART II

## NICK

The draft started and we've sat here anxiously waiting. I hold Amelia's hand tightly as she sits next to me. I have a smile on my face the whole time but my heart is beating a million beats per minute.

Roger Goodell steps onto the podium and announces the 15<sup>th</sup> pick of the first round. It's not me. With the Buffalo Bills on the clock, I close my eyes and take a deep breath.

I hear a buzzing sound and wonder where it's coming from. I look at the coffee table in front of me and notice it's my phone. My phone is ringing and it's a NY area code.

"Pick it up," Amelia urges me as the guys all stare at us.

I feel like I'm frozen. But I snap out of it seconds later when Amelia hands me the phone. "Hi, is this Nick Hunter?" the voice on the other end of the phone asks. I'm too nervous to try and figure out who it is.

"Yes," I reply. One word because I can't string more than that together right now.

"This is Sean McDermott from the Buffalo Bills. We're going to be selecting you with the 16th overall pick of the draft," he finishes.

The Buffalo Bills are selecting me. Holy crap. That means I'm only a few hours from my brother and Chase and Zack and home and everything. I worked out for them but I didn't think they'd choose me. Not because I'm not good enough but because I didn't think they'd choose a tight end so early. "Are you still there?" he asks.

"Yes sir," I tell him. "Thank you so much!"

He clears his throat. "We look forward to having you," he responds. "We'll be seeing you," he says.

"Thank you," I tell him.

"Take care," he says, then hangs up.

I look around the room at all my friends and family then my eyes land on Amelia. She looks at me with joy-filled eyes as she realizes that my dreams are coming true.

Everyone is silent. They don't say anything. They don't ask what the call is because they know better. They know what's about to happen.

"What now?" Amelia asks, confused.

"Just look at the screen," I tell her.


AMELIA


I LOOK AT HIM WITH PRIDE IN MY EYES. HE TOLD ME THE DAY OF THE championship game that he was playing for our baby. That our son was his motivation. He told me after winning that he wasn't going to let his son down. That every moment he was out on the field he was not playing for himself. He was playing for us.

I cried that night. Cried because he deserved to win. Cried

because he was thoughtful. Cried because he reminded me of what we had lost last year but also what we had gained, each other.

He tells me to look at the TV and I focus my attention on it. By now, the format is easy to follow. Goodell steps on the podium and announces which player each team is selecting.

The clock stops with a minute left to go and the Commissioner takes his place on the podium. "With the 16th Pick in the 2021 NFL Draft, the Buffalo Bills select Nick Hunter, #87, Bragan."

When the announcement is made, I jump out of the couch excitedly and scream. Let's just say I may not understand football very well but I support him.

Too quickly I realize that no one else is jumping up and down and I wonder why. I wonder if that's not what I'm supposed to do, though that's what all the other families on TV did. Turning to look at Nick, I'm immediately overcome by emotions.

"I always knew this was going to be one of the happiest days of my life," he says as he kneels on the floor in front of me.

I cover my mouth as the tears slide down my face. "What? What are...?" I start to speak then look around to find everyone smiling back at us.

"I've asked you to marry me many times before," he says. "I know you've always said no, so this is a big risk I'm taking," he says.

I laugh through the tears.

"But you gotta risk it to get the biscuit," he jokes, but I see the way his eyes begin to water.

I take deep breaths as I try to control my emotions.

"I'd risk it all for you, Amelia. I didn't know it then, but you're the one I've been waiting for. Will you marry me?"

I nod excitedly as he takes my hand and slides a gorgeous diamond ring onto my finger. I bring my arms around him and hug him tightly.

He stands up from the floor as he embraces me and everyone around us claps. "This was your moment," I tell him.

"And now I'll get to share it with you forever," he adds then kisses me like he's never kissed me before.

# ABOUT THE AUTHOR

Gianna Gabriela is a small town girl living in the Big Apple. Gianna's always been a writer. Growing up, she would write poems, speeches, and even songs. Still, one day she woke up with a pressing need to write a book. She heeded the desire and now writes stories featuring the brooding heroes you want and the strong heroines you need.

Keep up to date - sign up for Gianna's newsletter.
Feel free to text me: (917) 540-8167.

**Need more?**
**Here's what to read next...**

*Bragan University Series*

Better With You (Book #1)
Fighting For You (Book #2)
Falling For You (Book #3)
Better With You, Always (Book #4)

COMING SOON

Waiting For You (Book #5)
Finally With You (Book #6)

*The Not Alone Novellas*

Not the End (Book #1)
Not the Same (Book #2)

*Stand-Alone*

Just Because of You